SONGS FOR THE GUSLE

SONGS FOR THE GUSLE

Prosper Mérimée

Translated from the French

by

Laura Nagle

Frayed Edge Press
Philadelphia, PA

Published by Frayed Edge Press in 2023
First English Language Edition @2023 Frayed Edge Press

English Language Translation @2023 Laura Nagle

Frayed Edge Press
PO Box 13465
Philadelphia, PA 19101
http://frayededgepress.com

Library of Congress Control Number: 2022947907

Publisher's Cataloging-in-Publication Data

Names: Mérimée, Prosper, 1803-1870. La guzla... English. | Nagle, Laura, translator.
Title: Songs for the gusle / Prosper Mérimée ; translated by Laura Nagle.
Description: Philadelphia, PA : Frayed Edge Press, 2023. | First English language ed. |
Summary: First complete English-language translation of the purported collection of
    folktales, ballad lyrics, and travel narratives compiled and translated into French by an
    anonymous traveler returning from the Balkans. Later revealed to be a youthful hoax
    of the leading French Romanticist, Prosper Mérimée.
Identifiers: LCCN 2022947907 | ISBN 9781642510454 (pbk.) | ISBN 9781642510461
    (ebook)
Subjects: LCSH: French literature – 19th century. | Literary forgeries and mystifications
    – 19th century. | Balkan Peninsula – Folklore. | BISAC: FICTION / Fairy Tales, Folk Tales,
    Legends & Mythology. | FICTION / Satire. | FICTION / World Literature / France / 19th
    Century.
Classification: LCC PQ2362.G83 2023 | DDC 848 M47--dc23
LC record available at https://lccn.loc.gov/2022947907

Note: All footnotes in the following text appear in the source text and represent the narrator's voice.

No explanatory notes have been added by the translator or publisher in the main text.

CONTENTS

PREFACE TO THE FIRST EDITION

When I was compiling the collection of verse of which you are about to read the translation, I imagined myself to be just about the only Frenchman (for I was, at that time, a Frenchman) who could find anything of interest in these artless poems, the product of an uncultured people. The thought of publishing them, therefore, was far from my mind.

Since that time, observing the ever more prevalent appetite for foreign works, and especially for those that deviate, in their very forms, from the masterpieces we generally admire, I thought of my collection of Illyrian songs. I made a few translations of them for my friends, and it is on their advice that I venture to submit a selection thereof to public judgment.

I was, one might say, uniquely suited to this undertaking. In my younger years, I lived in the Illyrian Provinces. My mother was a Morlach from Spalato, and I long spoke Illyrian more often than Italian.[1] Having an innate love of travel, I used the time left over from my minor occupations to become well-acquainted with the country in which I was living; indeed, there is hardly a village, mountain, or valley between Trieste and Ragusa that I have not visited. I even made some rather lengthy excursions into Bosnia and Herzegovina, where the purity of the Illyrian tongue has been preserved. It was there that I discovered some rather curious fragments of old poetry.

Here, I must pause to address my choice of the French language for this translation. I am Italian; however, following certain events that occurred in my country, I now live in France, a country I have always loved and of which I was, for some time, a citizen. My friends are French, and I have come to consider France my homeland. I make no pretense of writing in French with the

---

1. The Morlachs are speakers of Slavic or Illyrian, residing in Dalmatia.

elegance of a man of letters; such pretension would be ludicrous indeed in a foreigner such as I! However, my education and long residence in this country have enabled me, I believe, to write with a certain facility—particularly in the case of a translation, whose principal concern, in my opinion, is exactitude.

Having been under French rule for a period of time, the Illyrian Provinces are familiar enough, I reckon, that this collection requires no geographic, political, or other descriptors by way of introduction.

I shall merely say a few words about the Slavic bards, or gusle players, as they are called.

The majority are impoverished old men, often dressed in rags, who roam about the towns and villages singing ballads and accompanying themselves on a guitar-like instrument called a gusle, which has but a single horsehair string. The idle (who are numerous, as the Morlachs have little taste for work) gather around, and when the ballad is finished, the performer awaits his recompense, which is left to the generosity of his audience. Sometimes, as a clever ruse, he pauses at the most crucial moment in his tale to appeal to the crowd's largesse; he will often go so far as to set a price for which he will agree to recite the denouement.

These men are not the only singers of ballads; nearly all the Morlachs, young and old alike, take part as well. Some of them, though very few, compose verses, often through improvisation (see the Biographical Note on Maglanović). Their singing style is nasal, and there is scant variation among the melodies. The gusle accompaniment does little to enhance them, and only habitual listening can make this music tolerable. At the end of each verse, the singer lets out a shriek akin to the howl of an injured wolf. These cries are audible even in the distant mountains, and only through familiarity does one come to recognize them as utterances from a human mouth.

1827.

BIOGRAPHICAL NOTE ON
HIJACINT MAGLANOVIĆ

Hijacint Maglanović is perhaps the only gusle player I've ever encountered who was also a poet. Most of them simply play old songs ad nauseam, or at most they compose pastiches, taking twenty lines or so from one ballad, the same number from another, and linking them together with some shoddy verse of their own creation.

Our poet was born in Zvonigrad, as he himself mentions in his ballad "The Veljko Hawthorn." He was a cobbler's son, and his parents do not appear to have taken great pains to educate him, as he can neither read nor write. At eight years of age, he was abducted by the "Tsiganes," or Bohemians, who took him to Bosnia. There, he was taught their ways and was easily converted to the Muslim faith, which most of them practice.[1] An *ayan*, or mayor, from Livno snatched him from their clutches and pressed the boy into his own service for several years.

He was fifteen years of age when a Catholic monk successfully converted him to Christianity. The monk had run the risk of being impaled if he were discovered, as the Turks do not welcome missionary work. The decision to leave a master who was rather harsh (as most Bosnians are) posed no dilemma for young Hijacint. As he made his escape, however, he sought to exact vengeance for his ill-treatment. He left Livno under cover of a stormy night, taking with him a pelisse, his master's saber, and the few sequins he was able to steal. The monk who had rebaptized him joined in his escape, which he had perhaps suggested in the first place.

The distance from Livno, Bosnia, to Sinj, Dalmatia, is but a dozen leagues or so. Before long, the fugitives arrived in Sinj, under

---

1. I learned all these details in 1817 from Maglanović himself.

the protection of the Venetian government and safe from the ayan's pursuit. It was in that town that Maglanović wrote his first song; he immortalized his escape in a ballad that attracted some admirers and through which he began to make a name for himself.[2]

But he had no other means of subsistence, and his character was such that he had little taste for work. He survived for a time on the Morlachian hospitality and charity of the country folk, earning his keep by singing and playing on the gusle one or another of the old tunes he knew by heart. Before long, he was composing his own ballads for weddings and funerals. He had such a knack for making himself indispensable that no good party could do without Maglanović and his gusle.

Thus he lived in the vicinity of Sinj, giving little thought to his kin. Indeed, he knows nothing of their fate; since his abduction, he has never returned to Zvonigrad.

At the age of twenty-five, he was a handsome man, strong and clever, a good hunter, and a famous poet and musician to boot; everyone thought well of him, especially the young ladies. His favorite, Helena, was the daughter of a wealthy Morlach named Zlarinović. He easily won her over and, in keeping with custom, abducted her, that they might elope. His rival was a sort of local nobleman by the name of Ugljan, who learned of the planned abduction. According to Illyrian custom, rejected lovers are readily consoled and no longer look askance at their more fortunate rivals; but this Ugljan, in a fit of jealousy, took it into his head to put up an obstacle to Maglanović's happiness. On the night of the abduction, just as Helena found herself mounted on a horse and prepared to follow her lover, Ugljan arrived with two of his servants and shouted menacingly at them to halt. The two rivals took up their arms. Maglanović shot first and killed Lord Ugljan. Had he a family to join in his feud, he would not have left the country over such a trifling matter; but he had no relations to help him, leaving him alone exposed to the vengeance of Ugljan's entire clan. He quickly

---

2. I have tried in vain to obtain it. Maglanović himself has forgotten it—or, perhaps, was too ashamed to sing his earliest poetic effort for me.

came to a decision and fled with his wife to the mountains, where he joined forces with the hajduks.[3]

He long lived among them; he even sustained a facial wound in a skirmish with the pandours.[4] Finally, having earned some money by what I suspect were rather questionable means, he left the mountains, purchased some livestock, and came to settle in the Gorski Kotar region with his wife and several children. His house is located near Smoković, alongside a small river or large stream that flows into Lake Vrana. His wife and children look after their cows and their little farm, but he travels constantly. He often goes to visit with his old friends the hajduks, but he no longer takes part in their perilous trade.

I saw him for the first time in Zara, in 1816. I was, at the time, an Illyrian language enthusiast, and I greatly desired to hear a poet of renown. My friend, the esteemed voivode Nikola [*surname redacted*], had, near his home in Biograd, met with his acquaintance Hijacint Maglanović, and, aware that he was going to Zara, gave him a letter addressed to me. In order to make anything of the experience, he told me, I'd need to get him to drink, as inspiration came to him only when he was tipsy.

At the time, Hijacint was nearly sixty years of age. He was a tall man, spry for his age, with a solid build, broad shoulders, and a remarkably thick neck. His weather-beaten face; his small, somewhat Chinese-looking, upturned eyes; his Roman nose, made ruddy due to his consumption of hard liquor; and his long white mustache and heavy black eyebrows all made for an overall impression that, once seen, was not easily forgotten. Add to this a long scar that extended over the eyebrow and part of the cheek. (It is truly a wonder that he did not lose an eye when he was thus wounded.) His head was shaven, in keeping with the nearly universal Morlachian custom; he wore a black sheepskin cap and clothes that were in still in very good condition despite their age.

---

3. A kind of outlaw.

4. Members of the constabulary. See subsequent footnotes.

He entered my room and unceremoniously handed me the voivode's letter. When I had finished reading it, he said, "You speak Illyrian, then, do you?" in a tone that conveyed scornful doubt. I immediately replied, in that language, that I understood it well enough to appreciate his songs, of which I had heard the highest of praise. "Very well," said he, "but I am hungry and thirsty; I shall sing once I have had my fill." We dined together. He ate so greedily that it seemed to me he must have been fasting for at least four days. Following the voivode's counsel, I took care to see that he drank; my friends, having heard tell of his arrival, came to join us and kept his glass filled to the brim at all times. Our hope was that, once his extraordinary hunger and thirst were appeased, our man would be so kind as to sing a few of his tunes for us. Alas, our hopes were dashed. He abruptly rose from the table and curled up on a rug near the fire (it was December), and within five minutes he fell into a deep sleep from which he could not be roused.

On a different occasion, I was more fortunate: I took care to have him drink just enough to enliven him, and he sang to us several of the ballads you'll find in this collection.

His voice must have been beautiful once, but by that time it was a bit hoarse. As he sang along with his gusle, though, his eyes sparkled and his countenance took on the kind of rugged beauty that any painter should like to immortalize on canvas.

After staying at my home for five days, he took his leave in a most peculiar manner. One morning he went out, and I waited in vain for him until nightfall. I subsequently learned that he had left Zara to return home. At the same time, I also discovered that a pair of English pistols, which had been hanging in my bedroom prior to his precipitous departure, were now missing. To his credit, however, I must note that he could just as well have made off with my purse and a gold watch; taken together, they were ten times more valuable than the pistols.

In 1817, I spent two days at his home, where he greeted me with every sign of keen delight; likewise, his wife and all his children and grandchildren threw their arms around my neck. And when I left, his eldest son guided me for several days through the mountains and refused to accept any compensation for his services.

THE VELJKO HAWTHORN[5]

1

"The Veljko Hawthorn," by Hijacint Maglanović, a native of Zvonigrad, the most skillful of gusle players. Lend your ear!

2

The bey Ivan Veljko, son of Aleksej, left his home and his native land. His enemies came from the east; they burned down his house and usurped his land.

3

The bey Ivan Veljko, son of Aleksej, had twelve sons, of whom five died at the Obravo ford and five perished on the Rebrovje plain.

4

The bey Ivan Veljko, son of Aleksej, had a beloved son. They took him to Kremen; they shut him away in a prison and boarded up the door.

5

However, the bey Ivan Veljko, son of Aleksej, did not die fording the Obravo or on the Rebrovje plains, for he was too old to go to war, and he was blind.

---

5. The justification for this title appears only in the final stanza. The hawthorn, it seems, was the distinctive or heraldic symbol of the Veljko clan.

6

And his twelfth son did not die fording the Obravo or on the Rebrovje plains, for he was too young to go to war; he was barely weaned.

7

The bey Ivan Veljko, son of Aleksej, and his son crossed the yellow waters of the Mrežnica. To Đurađ Stipanić, he said, "Cover me with your coat, that I might sit in the shade."[6]

8

And so Đurađ Stipanić covered him with his coat; he ate bread and salt with the bey Ivan Veljko,[7] and when his wife bore him a son, he named the boy Ivan.[8]

9

But Nikola Janjevo, Josif Spalatin, and Fedor Aslar gathered in Kremen over the Easter holiday, and they ate and drank together.

10

And Nikola Janjevo said, "The Veljko clan has been decimated." And Josif Spalatin said, "Our enemy, Ivan Veljko, son of Aleksej, is still living."

---

6. This is a way of saying, *grant me your protection.*

7. In the Levant, of course, two people who have eaten bread and salt in one another's company are considered friends on the basis of that fact alone.

8. There is no greater token of one's esteem than naming someone godfather to a child.

11

And Fedor Aslar said, "Đurađ Stipanić covered him with his coat. He is leading a peaceful life on the other side of the Mrežnica with his youngest son, Aleksej."

12

The three men said, "Death to Ivan Veljko and to his son, Aleksej!" And they joined hands and drank plum brandy from the same goblet.[9]

13

On Whit Monday, Nikola Janjevo went down into the Rebrovje plains, followed by twenty men armed with sabers and muskets.

14

Josif Spalatin went down the same day with forty hajduks,[10] and Fedor Aslar joined them with forty horsemen wearing black sheepskin hats.

15

They passed by the Majavoda pond, where the water is black and there are no fish; they dared not let their horses drink from it, but watered them at the Mrežnica River.

---

9. Šljivovica.

10. Hajduks are an itinerant class of Morlach. They make their living by robbing and looting. The term is derived from the word *hayduk*, meaning "party leader."

16

"Beys from the East, what brings you here? What brings you to the land of Đurađ Stipanić? Are you going to Senj to congratulate the new potestate?"

17

"No, son of Stipan, we are not going to Senj," Nikola Janjevo replied. "We are trying to find Ivan Veljko and his son. There are twenty Turkish horses in it for you, if you hand those men over to us."

18

"I would not deliver Ivan Veljko to you for all the Turkish horses you own. He is my guest and my friend. My only son bears his name."

19

Then Josif Spalatin said, "Bring us Ivan Veljko, or blood will be spilled. We have come from the east astride our war horses; our weapons are loaded."

20

"I will not deliver Ivan Veljko to you, but if you must have blood, up on that mountain are a hundred and twenty horsemen, ready to descend at the first sound of my silver whistle."

21

Then, without a word, Fedor Aslar raised his saber and split the man's head in two, and they went into Đurađ Stipanić's house and there found his wife, who had witnessed this.

22

"Run for your life, son of Aleksej! Run for your life, son of Ivan! The beys from the East have killed my husband; they will kill you as well!" Thus spoke Teresa Gelin.

23

But the old bey said, "I am too old to run." He told her, "Save Aleksej, for he is the last of his name!" And Teresa Gelin said, "Yes, I will save him."

24

The beys from the East saw Ivan Veljko and cried out, "Death to him!" All at once their bullets flew and their sharp sabers cut short his gray hair.

25

"Teresa Gelin," they asked, "is this boy the son of Ivan?"[11] And she replied, "You shall not spill the blood of an innocent boy." And together they cried, "This is the son of Ivan Veljko!"

---

11. To make this stanza more intelligible, one would need to add: *they said, pointing at the son of Đurađ Stipanić.*

26

Josif Spalatin wished to abduct the boy; but Fedor Aslar pierced his heart with his yataghan,[12] killing the son of Đurađ Stipanić, believing him to be Aleksej Veljko.

27

And yet, ten years later, Aleksej Veljko had become a strong and skillful huntsman. One day he asked Teresa Gelin, "Mother, why are those bloodied gowns hanging on the wall?"[13]

28

"This one," she said, "is the gown of your father, Ivan Veljko, whose death has still not been avenged; and that one belonged to Đurađ Stipanić, whose death has not been avenged because he did not leave any sons."

29

The huntsman grew sad; no more did he drink plum brandy. Instead, he purchased gunpowder in Senj and gathered a group of hajduks and horsemen.

30

On Whit Monday, he crossed the Mrežnica, and he saw the pond where the water is black and there are no fish. There he came upon the three beys from the East as they sat eating.

---

12. A long Turkish knife with a slight curve and a sharp interior blade.

13. As per Illyrian custom.

31

"My lords! my lords!" a voice rang out. "Armed horsemen and hajduks are approaching astride glistening steeds. They have just forded the Mrežnica. It is Aleksej Veljko!"

32

"That is a lie, you old gusle scraper," came the response. "Aleksej Veljko is dead; I myself stabbed him with my dagger." But Aleksej appeared and cried out, "I am Aleksej, son of Ivan!"

33

Nikola Janjevo was killed by a bullet, and Josif Spalatin was killed by a bullet as well; but Aleksej cut off Fedor Aslar's right hand and then his head.

34

"Take down those bloodied gowns. The beys from the East are dead; Ivan and Đurađ have been avenged. The Veljko hawthorn blossoms once more; never shall its stems perish!"[14]

---

14. For the Morlachs, vengeance is a sacred duty. Indeed, their favorite proverb is: *He who goes unavenged is not blessed.* In the Illyrian tongue, the proverb (*Ko ne se osveti onse ne posveti*) involves a certain play on words; *osveta*, in Illyrian, means both "vengeance" and "sanctification."

The Death of Stjepan Tomašević, King of Bosnia[15]

Fragment

....

............Then the infidels cut off their heads. They saw Stjepan's head on the end of a lance, and a Tatar brought it over to the wall, shouting, "Stjepan Tomašević, behold the head of your son! As we have done to your son, so we shall do to you!" And the king rent his gown and lay himself down among the ashes, and he refused to eat for three days . . .

And the walls of Ključ were so riddled with cannonballs that they resembled a honeycomb; and not a soul dared glance upward as the arrows and cannonballs continued to rain down, killing and wounding Christians. And the Greeks[16] and those who went by the name of *God-pleasers*[17] betrayed us; they surrendered to Mehmed

---

15. Tomaš, King of Bosnia, was assassinated in secret, in 1460, by his two sons, Stjepan and Radivoj. The former—the hero of this ballad—succeeded him under the name Stjepan Tomašević. Radivoj, incensed at his exclusion from the throne, revealed the crime that he and Stjepan had committed, then sought refuge with Mehmed.

The Bishop of Modruš, the papal legate in Bosnia, persuaded Stjepan Tomašević that the best way to make amends for his patricide was to wage war against the Ottomans. This proved disastrous for the Christians: Mehmed laid waste to the kingdom and led a siege against Stjepan Tomašević at Ključ fortress in Croatia, where he had taken refuge. The sultan, finding that his forces were too slow in advancing toward his objective, proposed a truce with Stjepan Tomašević, on one condition: payment of the old tribute. Stjepan Tomašević, already in dire straits, accepted these terms and went to the infidels' camp. He was immediately detained and, when he refused to undergo circumcision, the barbaric conqueror had him first skinned alive, then finished off with arrows.

This is a very old piece, and I was able to obtain no more than this fragment of it. The beginning appears to refer to a battle lost by Stjepan Tomašević, son of King Tomaš, prior to the capture of Ključ fortress.

16. In Dalmatia and Bosnia, the Greek Orthodox and the Roman Catholics treat their condemnation of one another as a sort of competition. Each group refers to the other as *pasa vjerro*, or "dog faith."

17. In Illyrian, *bogou-mili*, the name the Paternians gave themselves. Their heresy was threefold: they regarded mankind as the work of the devil, rejected nearly every book of the Bible, and forswore priests.

and set to work undermining the walls. And yet those dogs, fearful of our sharp sabers, dared not storm the fortress. But that night, as the king lay sleepless in his bed, a ghost emerged through the floorboards of his chamber and said, "Stjepan, do you know me?" And the king trembled as he replied, "I do. You are my father, Tomaš." With that, the ghost held out its hand and shook its bloody gown over the king's head. And the king said, "When will you cease to trouble me?" And the ghost replied, "When you have given yourself over to Mehmed..."

And so the king entered Mehmed's tent. That demon glared at him with his evil eye[18] and said, "Have yourself circumcised or you shall perish." But the king proudly replied, "By the grace of God, I have lived as a Christian, and as a Christian shall I die." With that, the evil infidel had him seized by his executioners. They skinned him alive and fashioned a saddle from his skin. Then, their archers took him as their target, and he died a miserable death as a result of his father's curse.

---

18. To this day, the Greeks hold that the sultan Mehmed II was none other than the devil incarnate.

The Vision of Stjepan Tomašević, King of Bosnia[19]

By Hijacint Maglanović

1

King Stjepan Tomašević paced in his chamber, taking long strides, as his soldiers lay asleep with their heads over their weapons; but the King was unable to sleep, for the infidels were laying siege to his city, and Mehmed sought to send his head to the great mosque in Constantinople.

2

And he leaned out the window to listen for any bit of noise, but he heard only the owl above the palace; she wept, for soon she would need to seek another dwelling place for her young.

3

But it was not the owl causing this foreign sound, and it was not the moon illuminating the stained-glass windows of the Ključ church; no, there were drums and trumpets sounding in the Ključ church, and torches had turned night into vivid day.

4

And all around the great King Stjepan Tomašević, his loyal servants lay sleeping, and no ear but his own had heard this dreadful noise.

---

19. See the footnote to the previous ballad for a summary of the events that led to the conquest of the Kingdom of Bosnia.

He alone emerged from his chamber, saber in hand, for he had seen in the sky an omen of the future.

5

It was with a steady hand that he opened the church door, but as he beheld what lay in the choir, his courage all but failed him. Holding a proven amulet in his left hand, he felt heartened as he entered the great church of Ključ.

6

And the vision he saw there was strange indeed: the stone floor of the church was littered with the bodies of the dead, their blood gushing like the torrents that flow each autumn from the Prologh Mountains into the valleys below. Once inside the church, he had to step over corpses, ankle-deep in their blood.

7

And those bodies were the bodies of his loyal servants, and that blood was the blood of Christians. A cold sweat trickled down his back, and his teeth chattered at the horror all around. In the choir, he saw armed Turks and Tatars alongside those turncoats, the *bogou-mili*![20]

8

And beside the desecrated altar stood Mehmed, he of the evil eye, his saber red from tip to hilt; and standing before him was Tomaš I,[21] who was bending the knee and humbly presenting his crown to the foe of Christendom.

---

20. The Paternians.

21. King Tomaš, father of Stjepan Tomašević.

9

Kneeling by his side was the traitor Radivoj,[22] a turban on his head. In one hand he held the rope he had used to strangle his father, and in the other he grasped the caftan of the vicar of Satan,[23] leaning over to kiss it, in the manner of a slave who has just been cudgeled.

10

And Mehmed deigned to smile. He took the proffered crown, then shattered it beneath his feet. "Radivoj," he declared, "I grant you my Bosnia to govern, and I desire that those dogs name you their beylerbey."[24] And Radivoj prostrated himself and kissed the blood-soaked ground.

11

And Mehmed summoned his vizier and said, "Vizier, let a caftan be given to Radivoj.[25] The caftan he shall wear shall be more precious than Venetian brocade: for it is none other than the skin of Stjepan Tomašević that his brother shall don." And the vizier replied, "To hear is to obey."[26]

12

And the good king Stjepan Tomašević felt the hands of the infidels rending his clothing, and their yataghans cleaving his skin. With

---

22. His brother, who had helped him commit patricide.

23. Mehmed II.

24. This word, meaning "lord of lords," is the title of the Bosnian pasha. Radivoj never did assume that position, and Mehmed was careful not to leave a single member of the royal family in Bosnia.

25. The great lord presents a lavish caftan or pelisse to dignitaries when they are about to take control of their administrations.

26. The standard response of Ottoman slaves upon receiving an order.

their fingers and their teeth they pulled at his skin, extracting it all down to the toes,[27] and Radivoj cheerfully donned that skin.

13

Then Stjepan Tomašević cried out, "You are just, O Lord, to punish a patricide! Dispose of my body as You will; but, heavenly Jesus, I pray, have mercy on my soul!" At the sound of the holy name, the church shook, the ghosts vanished, and the torches all at once went out.

14

Have you ever seen a bright star dash across the sky and cast its light upon the earth in the distance? Before long, that shooting star disappears into the night, and the shadows return, darker still than before; and thus vanished the vision of Stjepan Tomašević.

15

He felt his way back to the church door; the air was clear and, all around, the rooftops glowed in the moonlight. All was still, and perhaps the king was given to believe that peace still reigned in Ključ, until a bomb launched by the infidel fell before him and heralded the attack.[28]

---

27. Stjepan Tomašević was, in fact, skinned alive.

28. Maglanović had seen bombs and mortars, but did not realize that these instruments of destruction were invented long after the time of Mehmed II.

THE MORLACH IN VENICE[29]

1

When Praskovia had deserted me, when I was sad and penniless, a wily Dalmatian came to my mountain and said these words to me: "Go to that great City of Water, for there, sequins are more abundant than stones are in your country.

2

"The soldiers are clad in silk and gold, and they pass their time indulging in all manner of pleasures. After you have earned money in Venice, you shall return to your country with a gold-tasseled waistcoat and silver chains upon your khanjar.[30]

3

"And then—think of it, Dmitri!—what young lady could resist calling to you from her window and throwing her bouquet to you when you have tuned your gusle? Take to the sea and come to the big city; believe me, you are certain to make your fortune."

---

29. The Republic of Venice maintained a corps of soldiers known as *stratioti*. The troops comprised a mishmash of Morlachs, Dalmatians, and Albanians. Like all military entities in Venice, they were regarded with disdain. The subject of this ballad appears to be a young Morlach who was unlucky in love and enlisted in a moment of chagrin.

The presence of some outdated expressions suggests that this is a very old tune, one that precious few old men can still imbue with meaning. For that matter, it is commonplace to hear a gusle player sing words he could not possibly explain. They learn by heart at a tender age, rehearsing their fathers' songs the way a parrot repeats its lesson. Sadly, it is quite rare these days to find Illyrian poets who do not copy others, but make the effort to preserve this beautiful language, the use of which is dwindling day by day.

30. A large knife that can serve as a dagger if need be.

4

Fool that I was, I believed him, and I came to this great vessel of stone; but the air here suffocates me, and their bread is poison to me. I cannot go where I please, cannot do as I please; I am like a dog on a leash.

5

The women laugh in my face when I speak in the language of my country. Here, our mountain folk have forgotten their native tongue and our old customs. Like a tree transplanted in the summer heat, I am withering and dying.

6

On my mountain, any time I encountered a man he would greet me with a smile, saying, "God be with you, son of Aleksej!" But here I find no friendly faces. Here I am like an ant flung by the breeze into the middle of a vast pond.

Death Song[31]

1

Farewell, farewell, good journey to you! The moon is full tonight; you'll find your way by its light. Good journey to you!

2

A bullet is preferable to the fever: free you lived and free you died. Your son Ivan has avenged you; he has killed five of them.

3

We drove them out of Kapelica all the way to the plains, and not a single one dared look over his shoulder for a final glance at us.

4

Farewell, farewell, good journey to you! The moon is full tonight; you'll find your way by its light. Good journey to you!

5

Tell my father that I am well, that I no longer feel the effects of my injury, and that my wife Helena has given birth to a son.[32]

---

31. Maglanović improvised this song at the burial of a relative of his, a hajduk who had run afoul of the law and been killed by the pandours.

32. Relatives and friends always give the deceased messages to pass along in the next world.

6

I named the boy Vladan after him. When my son is grown, I will teach him to fire a rifle and carry himself like a brave warrior.

7

Crusić ran off with my eldest daughter, and now she is six months along. I hope she will give birth to a strong, handsome boy.[33]

8

Tvrtko left our country and took to the sea; we have heard no more from him. Perhaps you will meet him in the land to which you are going.

9

You have a saber, a pipe and tobacco, and a goat's hair coat: all you need for a long journey to a place with neither cold nor hunger.[34]

10

Farewell, farewell, good journey to you! The moon is full tonight; you'll find your way by its light. Good journey to you!

---

33. A father never quarrels with his daughter's abductor—provided, of course, that all transpires without violence. (See *Danisić's Betrothed*, footnote 1).

34. Hajduks are buried with their weapons and pipe, as well as the clothing they were wearing when they died.

LORD MERCURIUS

1

The infidels penetrated our country, seeking to abduct our women and children. They put the little children in front of them on their saddles; as for the unfortunate women, each of them was carried on a horse's hindquarters, one of her fingers between an infidel's teeth.[35]

2

Lord Mercurius raised his banner as his three nephews and thirteen cousins lined up around him, each of them bearing gleaming weapons, with the holy cross and amulets worn over their clothing to protect them from misfortune.[36]

3

Once Lord Mercurius had mounted his steed, he spoke to his wife, Euphemia, who was holding the bridle, and said, "Take this amber rosary. If you are faithful to me, it shall remain intact; if you are untrue, the string shall break and the beads shall fall."[37]

---

35. This barbaric manner of transporting prisoners is common practice, particularly in the context of surprise attacks by the Arnauts. If their victim makes the slightest sound, the finger is bitten off. Based on this and other related remarks, I assume the author of this ballad is alluding to a war between the kings of Bosnia and the Muslims in ages past.

36. In general, these amulets are made from strips of paper on which various Gospel passages are written, mixed in with strange characters and shrouded in a red leather purse. The Morlachs place great faith in these talismans, known as *zapiz*.

37. The Illyrians' contempt for their wives is, as ever, in evidence here.

4

And so he set forth. Some time went by and no one received word from him. His wife feared him dead, or else captured by the Arnauts and taken to their country. But when three moons had passed, Spiridion Petrović returned.

5

He arrived in torn, blood-stained clothing, beating his chest. He said, "Your husband, my cousin, is dead; the infidels took us by surprise and killed him. I saw an Arnaut cut off his head. Only with great difficulty did I escape with my life."

6

With that, Euphemia cried out and rolled about on the ground, rending her garments. "But why," Spiridion asked, "are you so distressed? Are there no good men remaining in this land?" And the deceitful Spiridion helped her to her feet and consoled her.

7

Even as Mercurius's dog howled and his horse neighed, mourning their departed master, his wife, Euphemia, dried her tears and slept with the traitor Spiridion that very night. Now we shall leave this faithless woman and sing instead of her husband.

8

The king said to Lord Mercurius, "Go to the Fortress of Klis,[38] and tell the queen to come meet me at my camp." And Mercurius

---

38. Klis was frequently inhabited by the Bosnian kings, who were also in possession of large portions of Dalmatia.

set out at once, and he rode for three days and three nights without stopping.

9

And when he reached the banks of the Cetina, he ordered his squires to pitch his tent while he went down to the lake for a drink of water. But the lake was covered by a heavy mist, from which muffled cries could be heard.

10

And the water was rough, foaming like the Žemica whirlpool when it sinks beneath the earth. Once the moon had risen, the fog dispersed, revealing an army of little dwarfs galloping on horseback over the lake, as though it had frozen over.[39]

11

As they reached the shore, both the men and their steeds grew larger, reaching the size of the Duare mountain dwellers.[40] They lined up in formation and departed in an orderly fashion, then leapt joyfully across the plain.

12

And at times they faded to a misty gray, and one could see through their bodies to the grass beyond; and at other times their weapons gleamed, and their bodies appeared as though aflame. Suddenly a warrior emerged from the formation astride a black courser.

---

39. Tales of ghost armies are very common in the East. Moreover, everyone has surely heard of the night when ghosts laid siege to the city of Prague and a certain savant chased them off with a cry of "*Vezele, vezele!*"

40. They are known for their impressive stature.

13

And when he came before Mercurius, he performed a caracole and indicated his desire to fight. And so Mercurius made the sign of the cross, spurred his fine horse forward, and charged full speed, with his lance couched, toward the phantom.

14

Eight times they met in the field, and their lances yielded like iris leaves upon contact with their breastplates; but each time they met, Mercurius's horse fell to his knees, for the phantom's horse was by far the stronger of the two.

15

"Let us put our feet to the ground," said Mercurius, "and fight once more on foot." And so the phantom leapt from his horse and ran toward the brave Mercurius; but despite the phantom's size and great strength, he was felled by a single blow.

16

"Mercurius! Mercurius! You have vanquished me, Mercurius!" cried the phantom. "As tribute, I wish to offer you a word of warning: do not return home, for death awaits you there." The moon misted over, and the warrior and his army suddenly disappeared.

17

"He who attacks the devil," said Mercurius, "is a fool indeed. I vanquished a demon, and all I have to show for it is a horse with skinned knees and an ominous prophecy. Yet this shall not impede me from seeing my home and my dear wife, Euphemia, once more."

18

And that night, by the light of the moon, he arrived at the cemetery in Pakoštane.[41] There he saw priests and mourners, along with a chiaus,[42] standing around a freshly dug grave, beside which lay the deceased: a man with his saber by his side and a black veil over his head.

19

Mercurius pulled up his horse and called out, "Chiaus, whom would you bury there?" And the chiaus replied, "Lord Mercurius, who died today." Mercurius broke out in laughter at his reply; but the moon misted over once again, and he could see no more.

20

When he arrived home, he kissed his wife, Euphemia. "Euphemia," he said, "bring me the rosary that I gave you before I left; I would sooner place my trust in those amber beads than in a woman's vows." Euphemia said, "I will bring it to you."

21

The magic rosary had broken, but Euphemia had made another: identical to the first, but poisoned. "That is not my rosary," said Mercurius. "Count all the beads," his wife replied; "as you well know, there were sixty-seven of them."

---

41. Lord Mercurius's home must have been located in that village.

42. I believe this to be a loanword of Turkish origin, meaning "master of ceremonies."

22

And Mercurius counted the beads in his hands, licking his fingers from time to time, and the subtle poison slipped beneath his skin. When he arrived at the sixty-sixth bead, he heaved a great sigh and fell dead.

THE BRAVE HAJDUKS[43]

In a cave, the brave hajduk Kristijan Mladin lies on sharp pebbles. Beside him lies his beautiful wife, Katarina; at his feet, his two brave sons. For three days they have lain hungry in this cave, for their enemies lie in wait at every mountain pass; if they so much as raise their heads, a hundred rifles are pointed at them. They are so thirsty that their tongues are black and swollen, for they have naught to drink but a bit of stagnant water in the hollow of a rock. And yet not one of them has let out the slightest moan, for they fear Kristijan Mladin's displeasure.[44] When three days had passed, Katarina cried out, "May the Holy Virgin have mercy upon you, and may she take vengeance on your enemies!" Then she heaved a sigh and she was no more. Kristijan Mladin beheld his wife's corpse with a dry eye, and his two sons wiped away their tears when he was not looking. The fourth day dawned and the sun dried up the stagnant water in the hollow of the rock, whereupon Kristijan, the elder of Mladin's sons, went mad. Drawing his khanjar,[45] he looked upon his mother's corpse, his eyes akin to those of a wolf who spots a lamb. His younger brother Aleksandar, repulsed by what he saw, drew his own khanjar and pierced his own arm. "Drink my blood, Kristijan, and commit no offense.[46] When we all are dead of hunger, we shall return to suck our enemies' blood." Mladin

---

43. Hijacint Maglanović is said to have written this lovely ballad during the period when he himself was living the life of a hajduk, something more or less akin to a highwayman.

44. The Morlachs are known for their pain tolerance, but the hajduks are hardier still. I once saw a young man die; he had fallen from the top of a boulder, and his legs were broken in five or six places. As he lay in agony for three days, he did not utter a single moan. Even when an old lady who was said to have some medical knowledge tried to lift the man's broken limbs to apply some remedy or other, I only saw his fists tighten and his thick eyebrows draw closer in a way I found chilling.

45. The large knife that the Morlachs customarily carry at their waists.

46. This line is reminiscent of the famous phrase uttered by a Breton squire at the Combat of the Thirty: "Drink thy blood, Beaumanoir!"

arose and cried out, "On your feet, my children! Better to take a fine bullet than to suffer the agony of hunger." The three of them descended the mountain like rabid wolves. They killed ten men apiece; they each took ten bullets to the chest. Our cowardly foes cut off their heads and paraded them in triumph; but they hardly dared to look at them, such was their fear of Kristijan Mladin and his sons.[47]

---

47. The soldiers who fight the hajduks are known as pandours. Their reputation is hardly superior to that of the bandits they pursue; indeed, it is said that they often rob the very travelers they are sworn to protect. Furthermore, their cowardice makes them an object of scorn throughout the country. It is not uncommon for ten or twelve hajduks to escape the clutches of a hundred pandours. Granted, the unfortunate hajduks often endure hunger, which spurs them to bravery.

When the pandours take a prisoner, they have quite a unique way of transporting him. After confiscating his weapons, they simply cut the string that holds his underwear up and let it hang down around his knees. Thus the poor hajduk is forced to walk very slowly, for fear of falling on his face.

Danisić's Betrothed

1

Euzebije gave me a ring of chased gold,[48] and Vladimir gave me a red toque adorned with coins;[49] and yet, Danisić, I love you better than them both.

2

Euzebije has a curly black mane, and Vladimir's complexion is as fair as that of a young woman from the mountains; and yet, Danisić, to me you are handsomer than they.

3

When Euzebije kissed me I smiled, and when Vladimir kissed me his breath was as sweet as violets; but when Danisić kisses me,[50] my heart quivers with pleasure.

---

48. Prior to marriage, women receive gifts from all comers; this is without significant implications. It is common for a girl to have five or six admirers from whom she receives some sort of present on a daily basis, yet she is under no obligation to offer them anything but hope. Once this little game has played out for some time, the young lady's favorite suitor asks her permission to abduct her, and she always replies by indicating a time and place for the abduction. Moreover, the girl's reputation incurs no damage; indeed, half of all Morlachian marriages are arranged in this manner.

49. For women, a red toque is a symbol of virginity. Should a young lady, having gone astray, dare to appear in public with her red toque, she would risk having it snatched from her head by a priest and then having her hair shorn by one of her relatives as a mark of her disgrace.

50. This is the most common of greetings. When a young lady crosses paths with a man she has seen before, she approaches and kisses him.
If you go to the door of a house in search of hospitality, the owner's wife or eldest daughter comes to hold your horse by the bridle and kisses you as soon as your feet hit the ground. It is very pleasant to be welcomed in this manner by a young girl, but the same greeting from a married woman has its disadvantages. It must be understood that,

4

Euzebije knows many old songs, and Vladimir can draw a resonant tone from the gusle. I love to hear songs and gusle music, but they must be Danisić's songs and his gusle.

5

Euzebije called upon his godfather to ask for my hand, and tomorrow Vladimir shall send the priest to speak with my father;[51] but come stand beneath my window, Danisić, and I shall run away with you.

doubtless as a result of excessive modesty and contempt for the world, married women almost never wash their faces and thus are hideously unclean.

51. Doubtless for purposes of a marriage proposal as well.

Lovely Helena

Part the First

1

Gather around Ivan Bietko, all ye who wish to hear the woeful tale of the lovely Helena and of her husband, Teodor Konopka. Ivan Bietko is the best gusle player you have ever heard or, indeed, ever will hear.

2

Teodor Konopka was a daring huntsman in my grandfather's day, and it is from my grandfather that I heard this tale. He married the lovely Helena, who chose him over Piero Stamati,[52] for Teodor was handsome, whereas Piero was ugly and unkind.

3

One day, Piero Stamati came to Teodor Konopka's home and said, "Helena, is it true that your husband has departed for Venice, where he is to remain for one year?" — "It is true indeed," said she, "and I am much aggrieved, for I must remain all alone in this big house."

4

"Weep not, Helena, on account of your solitude. Someone will come to keep you company. Let me sleep with you and I will give

---

52. This is an Italian name. In Morlachian storytelling, great pleasure is taken in assigning the most despicable traits to Italian characters. *Pasa vjerro* (dog faith) and *lantzmanizka vjerro* (Italian faith) are synonymous insults.

you a handful of shiny sequins with which to adorn your jet-black hair."

5

— "Get thee behind me, villain!" Helena cried. — "Let me sleep with you," the evil Stamati repeated, "and I will give you a velvet gown with as many sequins as will fit in my hat."

6

— "Get thee behind me, villain," Helena cried again, "or I will tell my brothers of your treachery, and they shall see to your death." But Stamati was a pug-nosed, stunted little old man, while Helena was tall and strong.

7

She made good use of her height and strength, causing Stamati to fall backward. He went home in tears, staggering along on his buckling knees.

8

He sought out a godless Jew and asked him how he might take his vengeance on Helena. The Jew said to him, "Search beneath a tombstone until you find a black toad,[53] then bring it to me in a clay pot."

53　In every country, there is a popular belief that the toad is a venomous animal. In English history, for example, we find the tale of a king poisoned by a monk with ale in which he had drowned a toad.

9

Stamati brought him a black toad he found beneath a tombstone. The Jew poured water over the creature's head and named it John. What a crime, indeed, to give a black toad the name of such a great apostle!

10

Then they pierced the toad's flesh with the tips of their yataghans until a fine poison seeped from all the pricks in its skin. They collected that poison in a vial and forced the toad to drink it. Afterward, they let it lick a luscious piece of fruit.

11

And Stamati said to a young boy who was following him, "Take this fruit to the lovely Helena and tell her it is a gift from my wife." The young boy delivered the luscious fruit as he had been told, and the lovely Helena eagerly ate it whole.

12

When she had eaten that beautifully colored fruit, she suddenly became flustered, feeling as though a serpent were wriggling about in her belly.
Let all those who wish to hear the end of this tale make an offering to Ivan Bietko.

PART THE SECOND

1

When the lovely Helena had eaten that fruit, she made the sign of the cross, but that did nothing to assuage the sensation of something writhing in her belly. She called for her sister, who told her to drink some milk; even so, she continued to feel like a serpent.

2

Ere long her belly began to swell, each day a bit more than the last. Indeed, the women began to say, "Helena is with child; but how can that be, with her husband away? He left for Venice more than ten months ago."

3

And so great was the lovely Helena's shame that she dared not hold her head aloft, much less go out into the street. No, she did naught but sit and cry all through the day and all through the night. To her sister she would say, "What will become of me when my husband returns?"

4

Teodor Konopka, a year of his journey having passed, sought to return home. He boarded a gilded galley and happily returned to his country. His neighbors and friends went to meet him, dressed in their finery.

5

But he looked all through the crowd and did not see the lovely Helena. And so he asked, "What has become of the lovely Helena, my wife? Why is she not here?" His neighbors smirked and his friends' cheeks reddened, but not one of them replied.[54]

6

When he entered his home, he found his wife sitting upon a cushion. "Stand, Helena," he said. She stood and he saw her belly, which was quite round. "What can this mean?" he cried. "Helena, it has been more than a year since last I slept by your side!"

7

"I swear to you, my lord, on the Blessed Virgin Mary, I remained faithful to you. But a spell was cast upon me and it caused my belly to swell." But he did not believe her. He drew his saber and cut off her head with a single blow.

8

When her head had been cut off, he said, "That child in her treacherous belly is without fault. I shall tear it out of her and raise it. When I see whom it resembles, then I shall know the identity of its father, and I will kill that traitor."

8 (*Variant*[55])

When her head had been cut off, he said, "I shall tear the child from her treacherous belly and leave it to die, exposed, in the

---

54. This passage is notable for its simplicity and dynamic brevity.

55. I have heard both versions of this ballad sung.

countryside. Its father will come to collect it, and then I shall know and kill that traitor."

9

He cut open her lovely white body, finding within not a child, but a black toad. "Alas!" he cried. "Alas! What have I done? I killed the lovely Helena, who had not betrayed me. A spell truly was cast upon her with a toad!"

10

He picked up his beloved wife's head and kissed it. All of a sudden, that cold head opened its eyes, and with trembling lips, it said, "I am innocent, but I was bewitched out of vengeance using a black toad.

11

"Because I remained faithful to you, Piero Stamati cast a spell on me, with the aid of an evil Jew who lives in the valley of tombs." With that, the head closed its eyes and its tongue froze in place, never to speak again.

12

Teodor Konopka sought out Piero Stamati and cut off his head. He also killed the evil Jew and had thirty Masses said for the repose of his wife's soul. May God have mercy upon him and upon them all!

ON THE EVIL EYE

INTRODUCTION

Throughout the Levant, and particularly in Dalmatia, there is a widely held belief that certain individuals have the power to cast a spell with their eyes. The influence that the evil eye can have over a person is not to be underestimated. To lose at gambling, or to trip over a rock in one's path, would be a mild consequence; all too often, the unfortunate victim faints, falls ill, and soon wastes away to his death. On two occasions, I myself have encountered victims of the evil eye. In the Knin Valley, a young girl was approached by a man from the countryside, who asked her for directions. She looked at him, let out a cry, and fell, unconscious, to the ground. The stranger fled. I was some distance away and, initially believing that he had murdered the young girl, I ran to her aid, along with my guide. The poor child soon regained her senses and told us that the man who had spoken to her had the evil eye, which had bewitched her. She bade us take her to see a priest, who gave her some relics to kiss and hung around her neck a piece of paper, which had strange words written on it and was wrapped in silk. The young girl's courage was thus restored, and two days later, when I set out to continue on my journey, she was in the bloom of health.

On another occasion, in the village of Pakoštane, I saw a twenty-five-year-old man go pale and fall to the ground for fear of a very elderly hajduk who was looking at him. I am told that he was under the influence of the evil eye, but that it was not the fault of the hajduk, who had come by his evil eye naturally and who was, in fact, chagrined by his fearsome power. I attempted to conduct an experiment, with myself as the subject: I spoke to the hajduk and beseeched him to look at me for a moment. However, he refused to do so, and he appeared so distressed by my plea that

I had no choice but to relent. The man's face was repulsive, with huge, bulging eyes, which he tended to keep downcast. I have been given to understand, however, that when he carelessly fixed his gaze on a person, it was impossible for him to look away before his victim collapsed. The young man whose fainting spell I witnessed had regarded him with a grotesque, wide-eyed stare, displaying every sign of terror.

I have also heard old wives' tales of people with two pupils in each eye. Those individuals, in the opinion of the women who told me those stories, constitute the most formidable cases.

There are a variety of methods used to protect oneself from the evil eye, although nearly all of them are inadequate to the task. Some people carry animal horns on their person, while others carry pieces of coral, which they point at any person suspected of having the evil eye.

It is also said that, at the moment you realize the evil eye is directed upon you, you must either touch iron or throw coffee in the face of the person bewitching you. Sometimes firing a pistol in the air is enough to break the fatal spell. On many occasions Morlachs have opted for a more direct approach: aiming their pistol at the ostensible enchanter.

Another method of casting a spell is to heap praise upon a person or thing. Not everyone has this dangerous skill, of course, nor is it always exercised deliberately.

My experiences are far from unique; anyone who has traveled to Dalmatia or Bosnia has found himself in the same position. In a village on the banks of the Trebišnjica, the name of which I no longer recall, I saw a pleasant-looking little child playing in the grass in front of a house. I patted him on the head and praised him to his mother. She appeared unmoved by my courtesy and beseeched me to spit on her child's forehead. I was unaware, at the time, that this was the way to break a spell cast with words. I was shocked at her request and stubbornly refused. The woman was calling out to her husband to put a pistol to my throat and force me to comply, when my guide, a young hajduk, explained it to me.

"Sir," he said, "I have always known you to be a good and honest man. Why, then, would you not break a spell that, I am certain, you cast unintentionally?" I then understood the mother's obstinacy and hastened to satisfy her demand.

In sum, in order to understand this next ballad as well as several others, one must believe that certain people cast spells with their eyes and others with their words; that this devastating power is passed down from father to son; and, finally, that those thus enchanted—women and children, in particular—wither and die forthwith.

[illegible] gs [illegible] to [illegible] ally [illegible] to [illegible]
[illegible] admire [illegible] then come too the [illegible]
[illegible] demand.

[illegible] the [illegible] that our people [illegible] others with their words, that [illegible] passed [illegible] that those that [illegible] in particular [illegible] result.

Maksim and Zoja[56]

By Hijacint Maglanović

1

Oh, Maksim Duban! Oh, Zoja, daughter of Jelavić! May the holy mother of God reward your love! May you find bliss in Heaven!

2

When the sun had set in the sea, when the voivode had gone to sleep, then could the sweet sound of a gusle be heard beneath the window of the lovely Zoja, eldest daughter of Jelavić.

3

And the lovely Zoja hastened on tiptoe to open her window, and a tall young man sat on the ground sighing as he played a love song on his gusle.

4

And the darkest nights were those he preferred; but when the moon was full, he hid in the shadows, and none but Zoja could catch a glimpse of him beneath his black lambskin pelisse.

---

56. This ballad provides an idea of modern tastes. Here we see the first glimmer of affectation, coupled with the simplicity of old Illyrian poetry. Moreover, it is much admired and is considered among Maglanović's finest work. Perhaps one must take into account the Morlachs' immoderate taste for any hint of the supernatural.

5

And who was that sweet-voiced young man? Who could say? He came from afar, yet spoke our tongue; he was familiar to no one, and Zoja alone knew his name.

6

But no one, not even Zoja, had seen his face; for when dawn approached, he slung his rifle over his shoulder and set out into the forest to hunt game.

7

And he returned each time with the horns of a mountain goat, and said to Zoja: "Carry these horns with you, and may Mary preserve you from the evil eye!"

8

He wrapped a shawl around his head in the manner of the Arnauts,[57] and no wandering traveler who ever encountered him in the woods ever saw his face beneath the many folds of gilt muslin.

9

But one night, Zoja said, "Come near, that I might touch you." And with her pale hand she touched his face; and her own features felt no more beautiful than his.

---

57. In winter the Arnauts cover their ears, cheeks, and most of the face in a shawl wrapped around the head and chin.

10

And so she said to him, "I am grown weary of the young men of this country, all of whom pursue me; I love only you. Come tomorrow at noontime, when they will be at Mass.

11

"I shall mount your horse behind you, and you shall take me away to your country, to be your wife. Long have I worn opanci; I wish to have embroidered slippers."[58]

12

The young gusle player sighed and said, "What do you ask of me? I mustn't see you during the day; but come down this very night, and I shall take you away with me to the beautiful Knin valley, where we shall be wed."

13

"No," said she, "I want you to take me away tomorrow, for I wish to have my nice clothes, and my father has the key to the trunk. Tomorrow I shall steal it, and then I shall come with you."

14

He sighed again and said, "As you wish, so it shall be." Then he kissed her; but the roosters crowed, the sky grew pink, and the foreigner departed.

---

58. An allusion to the custom by which girls are required to wear this crude type of footwear prior to marriage. Later, they may wear slippers (*pashmak*), similar to those worn by Turkish women.

15

And when the noon hour arrived, he appeared at the voivode's door, astride a steed as white as milk; and on its haunches was a velvet pillow for sweet Zoja's comfort.

16

The foreigner's clothes gleamed with gold, and his belt was embroidered with pearls.[59] But his brow was hidden beneath a thick veil; barely were his mouth and mustache discernible.

17

And the lovely Zoja mounted nimbly behind him on his milky-white steed, who whinnied with pride at his burden and galloped away, leaving whirlwinds of dust in his wake.

18

"Tell me, Zoja, have you brought the fine horn that I gave to you?" — "No," she replied, "whatever would I do with such a trinket? I am bringing my gilt dresses, my necklaces, and my pendants."

19

"Tell me, Zoja, have you brought the fine relic that I gave to you?" — "No," she replied, "I hung it around my little brother's neck, that it might heal him, for he is ill."

---

59. This is the part of a man's attire on which he places an item of particular value.

20

And the foreigner sighed sadly. "Now that we are far from my home," said the lovely Zoja, "halt your fine horse, remove this veil, and let me kiss you, my darling Maksim."[60]

21

But he said, "Tonight we will be comfortably ensconced in my home, where there are satin cushions; tonight we will lie together beneath damask curtains."

22

"Alas!" cried the lovely Zoja, "is this the love you have for me? Why will you not turn your face toward me? Why do you treat me with such disdain? Am I not the most beautiful girl in the country?"

23

"Oh, Zoja!" said he, "someone could pass by and see us. Your brothers would chase after us and return us to your father." As he said this, he struck his steed with his whip.

24

"Stop! Stop, Maksim," she cried. "I see now that you do not love me. If you will not turn round to look at me, I will leap from this horse, even if doing so should kill me."

---

60. Here, one sees how the legend of Orpheus and Eurydice has been distorted by the Illyrian poet, who, I am certain, has never read Virgil.

25

And so the foreigner pulled up his horse with one hand, as with the other he threw his veil to the ground, and he turned himself round to kiss the lovely Zoja. But alas—Holy Mother of God!—he had two pupils in each eye![61]

26

Lethal was his gaze! Before his lips could meet those of the lovely Zoja, the young girl's head fell to her shoulder and she tumbled, pale and lifeless, from the horse.

27

"Cursed be my father," cried Maksim Duban, "who gave me this evil eye![62] I do not wish to cause further harm!" And with that, he gouged out his own eyes with his dagger.

28

He had the lovely Zoja buried with great ceremony; and as for himself, he entered a cloister. He did not remain there long; soon the lovely Zoja's tomb was opened once more and Maksim was laid by her side.

61. This is an unmistakable sign of the evil eye.

62. One must keep in mind that the evil eye is often hereditary.

THE EVIL EYE[63]

Refrain: Sleep peacefully, poor child, and may Saint Eusebius have mercy upon you!

1

Damned foreigner, may you perish between the teeth of a bear, and may your wife be unfaithful to you!
    [Refrain]

2

With flattering words he praised my child's beauty; he ran his hand through the boy's golden hair.
    [Refrain]

3

"Beautiful blue eyes," said he, "blue as a summer sky," and he stared into them with his own eyes of gray.
    [Refrain]

4

"Happy the mother," said he, "happy the father"; yet he sought to wrest their child from them.
    [Refrain]

---

63. See "On the Evil Eye: Introduction."

5

With words of affection he bewitched the poor boy, who now grows thinner by the day.

> [Refrain]

6

His blue eyes, which the foreigner lauded, were made dull by the words of power.

> [Refrain]

7

His golden hair has turned as white as an old man's, so potent were the spells.

> [Refrain]

8

If I could have my way with that damnable foreigner, I'd force him to spit on your beautiful forehead.

> [Refrain]

9

Take heart, child, for your uncle has gone to Stari Grad; he will bring back some earth from the saint's tomb.

> [Refrain]

10

And my cousin, the bishop, gave me a relic, which I shall hang around your neck to heal you.

> [Refrain]

THE FLAME OF PERUŠIĆ

BY HIJACINT MAGLANOVIĆ

1

Why is the bey Janko Marnavić absent from his country? Why does he roam the rugged mountains near Vrgorac, never spending two nights under the same roof? Is he hounded by his enemies? Have they sworn to pursue a blood feud with no end?

2

No. The bey Janko is wealthy and powerful. No man would dare proclaim himself Janko's enemy; at the mere sound of his voice, more than two hundred sabers would be unsheathed. Yet he seeks out deserted places and prefers to spend his time in hajduks' caves, for his heart succumbed to sorrow upon the death of his pobratim.[64]

---

64. Among the Morlachs, friendship is considered among the highest of honors. To this day, it is common to see two men enter into a commitment that might be considered a sort of chosen brotherhood. Illyrian rituals include prayers intended to solemnize the union of two friends who swear to aid and defend one another for the rest of their lives. In the Illyrian language, two men united by this religious ceremony are called *pobratimi*, and in the case of women, the term *posestrime* is used: literally, "half-brothers" or "half-sisters." Pobratimi sacrificing their lives for one another is a regular occurrence, and should they quarrel with one another, it would create as much of a scandal as if, in our culture, a son was seen to ill-treat his father. However, given the Morlachs' great fondness for strong liqueurs, and their habit of forgetting their vows of friendship under the influence thereof, their entourages must take great care to intercede between pobratimi and put a stop to any nascent quarrels; in a country where every man is armed, such disputes are, by their very nature, lethal.

On one occasion, in Knin, I witnessed a young Morlachian woman die of grief following the loss of her friend, who had, sadly, perished by falling from a window.

3

Ćiril Pervan died amidst a celebration, during which brandy flowed in abundance and the men went mad with drink. A dispute arose between two beys of great repute, and the bey Janko Marnavić shot his pistol at his enemy; but his hand was shaking from the brandy, and instead he killed his pobratim, Ćiril Pervan.

4

At the church in Perušić, they had sworn to live and die by one another's side; and yet, only two months after they took that vow, one of the pobratimi died at his brother's hand. Since that day, the bey Janko partook no more of wine and brandy; he ate naught but roots, and he ran about like an ox startled by a horsefly.

5

Finally, he returned to his country and walked into the church in Perušić. There, he spent an entire day praying as he lay on the floor, weeping bitter tears, his arms outstretched as though bound to a cross. But when night came, he returned to his home, and he appeared calmer; he ate the supper served to him by his wife and children.

6

And once he was in his bed, he called to his wife and asked, "From the mountain in Pristeg, can you see the church in Perušić?" She looked out the window and replied, "The Morpolača is shrouded in fog, and I cannot see anything on the other side." The bey Janko said, "Very well, lie down beside me again." And as he lay in his bed, he prayed for Ćiril Pervan's soul.

7

And having prayed, he said to his wife, "Open the window and look out in the direction of Perušić." His wife rose straightaway and said, "Amid the fog, I see, on the other side of the Morpolača, a faint flicker of light." With that, the bey smiled and bade his wife return to bed. He clutched his rosary and began to pray again.

8

Once he had said his rosary, he said to his wife, "Praskovia, open the window again and tell me what you see." And she rose from the bed and said, "My lord, I see in the middle of the river a bright light advancing rapidly to this side."[65] Then she heard a heavy sigh and the sound of something falling on the wooden floor. The bey Janko was dead.

---

65. It is a commonly accepted notion in Illyria (and among several other peoples as well) that a bluish flame flutters about gravesites, announcing the presence of the souls of the dead.

The style of this ballad is quite moving in its simplicity—a most unusual quality in the Illyrian poetry of our time.

Barcarolle

1

Pisombo, pisombo![66] The sea is blue, the sky is clear, the moon has risen, and the wind has ceased to swell our sails from above. Pisombo, pisombo!

2

Pisombo, pisombo! Let every man take up an oar and every oar be covered in white foam, and we shall arrive in Ragusa this very night. Pisombo, pisombo!

3

Pisombo, pisombo! Do not lose sight of the coast on the starboard side, for fear of pirates and their long boats laden with sabers and muskets.[67] Pisombo, pisombo!

4

Pisombo, pisombo! Here is the Chapel of Saint Stephen, patron of this ship.[68] O Great Saint Stephen, send us a breeze; we are weary of rowing. Pisombo, pisombo!

---

66. This word has no meaning. Illyrian seamen chant it continuously to keep time as they row.

Sailors of all nationalities have their own words or expressions to accompany their maneuvers.

67. Some of these boats can carry up to sixty men, and they are so narrow that the men cannot comfortably sit two abreast.

68. As a general rule, each vessel bears the name of the captain's patron saint.

5

Pisombo, pisombo! How well this handsome vessel responds to the rudder! I would not exchange it for a great carrack that takes seven days to go about.[69] Pisombo, pisombo!

---

69. This absurd joke is commonplace among seafaring peoples.

THE BATTLE OF ZENICA-VELIKA[70]

The great bey Radivoj led his brave men into battle against the infidels. When the Dalmatians beheld our yellow silk standards, they twirled their mustaches, pulled their caps down over their ears, and said, "We, too, wish to slay the infidels and bring their heads back to our country."[71] The bey Radivoj replied, "May God see to it!" We crossed the Cetina at once, and we burned down every town and village in which those circumcised dogs lived; and when we came upon Jews, we hanged them from the trees.[72] The beylerbey departed from Banja Luka with two thousand Bosnians to fight us;[73] but no sooner did their curved sabers glisten in the sun—no sooner had their horses neighed from atop the hill of Zenica-Velika—than the Dalmatians, craven wretches that they are, ran off and abandoned us. And so we gathered in a tight circle around the great bey Radivoj. "My Lord," one said, "we shall not leave you as those cowards did. With the help of God and the Holy Virgin, we shall return to our country and tell our children of this great battle." Then we smashed our scabbards.[74] Each member of our army fought with the valor of ten men, and our sabers ran red from hilt to tip. Alas, just as we prepared to cross back over the Cetina, the Silahdar Mohammed swooped down upon us with

---

70. I do not know the date of the event upon which this little poem is based. The gusle player who recited it for me was unable to give me any more information other than that it was a very old ballad and that his father had passed it down to him.

71. The Dalmatians are despised by the Morlachs, and the feeling is mutual. As the reader will soon discover, the author blames the loss of this battle on the Dalmatians' betrayal.

72. In that country, the Jews are despised by Christians and Turks alike, and they were treated most harshly in every war. They were, and remain to this day, as persecuted as the flying fish, to borrow Sir Walter Scott's ingenious analogy.

73. Banja Luka was for many years the residence of the beylerbey of Bosnia. Bosna-Seraj is the current capital of that pashalik.

74. An Illyrian custom, signifying a vow to conquer or die.

a thousand horsemen.[75] "My brave men," said the bey Radivoj, "those dogs are too great in number; there is no escape. Let those among us who are uninjured endeavor to reach the woods, where they might evade the Silahdar's cavalry." When he finished speaking, there were but twenty men remaining by his side, all of them his cousins; and so long as they survived, they defended their leader, the bey. When nineteen of them had been killed, the youngest among them, Tomaš, said to the bey: "Mount this snow-white horse and it will carry you across the Cetina, back to our country." But the bey refused to flee; instead, he sat cross-legged on the ground. That was when the Silahdar Mohammed came and severed his head.

---

75. The Turkish word silahdar, literally meaning "bearer of arms," designates one of the highest offices in a pasha's court.

On Vampirism

In Illyria, Poland, Hungary, Turkey, and parts of Germany, a forthright denial of the existence of vampires would leave a man vulnerable to accusations of irreligion and immorality.

The term "vampire" (in Illyrian, *vudkodlak*) is applied to any corpse that leaves its tomb, generally at night, and torments the living. Often, the vampire sucks the blood of the living from their throats, or else it might squeeze their throats, suffocating them. Those thus killed by a vampire become vampires themselves. It appears that vampires are stripped of any feelings of attachment; indeed, they have been seen to torment their friends and relatives, rather than strangers.

Some believe that a man becomes a vampire through divine punishment, while others consider it a matter of fate. The most widely accepted view is that schismatics and the excommunicated, when buried in holy ground (where they suffer great anguish, unable to find peace), take their vengeance on the living.

The signs of vampirism are as follows: the preservation of a corpse beyond the point at which other corpses begin to rot, fluidity of the blood, suppleness of the limbs, etc. It is also said that vampires keep their eyes open in their graves, and that their nails and hair continue to grow as in life. Some are recognizable by the noise they make in their tombs as they chew on whatever is nearby—in many cases, their own flesh.

These phantoms' apparitions cease only when they are exhumed and beheaded and their bodies burned.

The most common remedy for an initial vampire attack is to rub the entire body, especially the part that was bitten, with a combination of the blood that flows in the vampire's veins and the earth from around its grave. The wounds from a vampire bite appear as a small, bluish or reddish blotch, not unlike the mark left by a leech.

The following is a selection of vampire stories recounted by Dom Augustin Calmet in the second volume of his *Treatise on the Apparition of Spirits, Vampires, etc.*:

In early September, in the village of Kisiljevo, three leagues from Gradište, an old man died at age sixty-two. Three days after he was buried, he appeared to his son in the dark of night and asked for something to eat; once served, he ate and disappeared. The next day, the son told his neighbors what had happened. The father did not appear that night, but the following night he once again made himself visible and asked for something to eat. It is unknown whether his son gave him food or not, but in any case, the son was found dead the next day in his bed. That same day, five or six people in the village suddenly fell ill; and in a matter of days, they all died, one after the other.

The local officer or bailiff, once notified of these events, sent an account thereof to the court in Belgrade, which sent two officers and an executioner to the village to investigate the matter. The imperial officer, from whom we have this account, traveled there from Gradište to bear witness to this phenomenon, of which he had so often heard tell.

The tombs of all those who had died in the previous six weeks were opened. When they arrived at the old man's tomb, they found him with his eyes open and vermilion in color. He breathed normally, yet was as motionless as a corpse. From this, they concluded that he was the very exemplar of a vampire. The executioner drove a stake into his heart. A pyre was erected and the corpse was reduced to ashes. No sign of vampirism was ever found in his son's body, nor in any of the other corpses.

Roughly five years ago, a certain hajduk by the name of Arnold Paul, then living in Medveđa, was crushed to death by a falling hay cart. Thirty days after his death, four people died suddenly, in the manner in which, according to local tradition, the victims of vampires generally die. That was when people recalled the old tale Arnold Paul had often told: in the vicinity of Kaševar and along the border of Ottoman Serbia, he had been tormented by a Turkish vampire. (The local people also believe that those who were passive vampires in life become active vampires in death; in other words, those whose blood has been sucked in turn become bloodsuckers themselves.) He claimed to have found a way to heal himself, by eating some dirt from the vampire's sepulcher and dabbing the vampire's blood on himself. That precaution did not prevent him from becoming a vampire after he died, however; when his body was exhumed, forty days after burial, his corpse displayed all the signs of an archvampire. His body was vermilion in hue; his hair, nails, and beard had grown, and all his veins were filled with fluid blood, which flowed from every part of his body onto the shroud wrapped around him. The hadnagy (the local official) in whose presence the exhumation took place was an expert in matters vampirical. As is customary, he plunged a sharpened stake into the heart of the corpse, driving it through the body from front to back—which, they say, caused the body to emit a dreadful cry, as though Arnold Paul were still among the living—and then the body was decapitated and burned. The same process was then repeated upon the corpses of the four other people who had died from the effects of vampirism, for fear that they might in turn kill others.

Nevertheless, despite thus dispatching the corpses, late last year (in other words, after a period of five years), these deadly phenomena began to occur once more, and several residents of that same village sadly perished. In the space of three months, seventeen people—men and women, boys and girls of various ages—died of vampirism; some never showed signs of illness, while others expired after languishing for two or three days. Among these was a girl named Stanojka, daughter of the hajduk Stoiljković, who had gone to bed in perfect health, only to awaken in the middle of the night trembling, letting out dreadful cries, and saying that the hajduk Miloje's son—some nine weeks dead—had all but strangled her in her sleep. From that moment forward, she simply wasted away, and in three days' time she died. What that girl had said of Miloje's son caused him to be reputed as a vampire; he was exhumed and found to be so. The local chiefs, doctors, and surgeons examined how vampirism could have resurged after the precautions that had been taken some years earlier.

It was finally discovered, following considerable research, that the late Arnold Paul had killed not only the four people mentioned earlier, but also several cattle, which had been eaten by these new vampires, Miloje's son among them. Based on these indicators, it was decided that all those who had died within a certain period of time were to be disinterred. Of the forty or so bodies dug up, seventeen were found to display all the most obvious signs of vampirism; their hearts were duly run through, their heads cut off, their bodies burned, and their ashes disposed of in the river.

All the actions recounted here were conducted legally and in due form, and were attested to by several officers stationed in those parts, by the surgeons major of the regiments, and by esteemed local residents. The formal statement was sent late last January to the Imperial War Council in Vienna, which had established a military commission to investigate the truthfulness of these events.

I will close by recounting a similar event that I myself witnessed. I will leave it to my readers to draw their own conclusions.

In 1816, I had set out on foot for a journey around Vrgorac, and I was staying in the little town of Vrboska. My host was a Morlach who was quite rich by local standards: a most jovial man—and, not incidentally, a bit of a drunkard—by the name of Vuk Poglonović. His wife was young and still pretty, and his sixteen-year-old daughter was quite charming. I wanted to spend a few days at his home so I could sketch some ancient ruins in the area, but I found it impossible to rent a room from him in exchange for money; he insisted on having me as a guest. The price of my lodging, then, was a rather onerous display of gratitude, inasmuch as I had to hold my own with my friend Poglonović for as long as he wished to remain at the table. Anyone who has dined with a Morlach will understand what a trial that can be.

One evening, about an hour after the two ladies had left us, I was singing some local tunes to my host (as a ruse to avoid drinking any more), when we were interrupted by dreadful shrieks coming from the bedroom. Generally speaking, there is only one such room in the house, and it is shared by everyone. We ran, armed, to the bedroom, where a ghastly spectacle awaited us. The mother, pale and frenzied, was holding the body of her daughter. The girl, having fainted, was paler still than her mother and was laid out on the bale of straw that served as her bed. The mother cried out, "A vampire! A vampire! My poor daughter is dead!"

Together, we managed to help Chava come to. She told us that she had seen the window open and that a pale man wrapped in a shroud had thrown himself upon her and bitten her while attempting to strangle her. When she cried out, the specter fled and she fainted. However, she believed she recognized the vampire as a local man named Wiecznany, who had died more than a fortnight earlier. She had a small, red mark on her neck; I didn't know whether it was a beauty spot or if she had been bitten by some insect while she was having her nightmare.

When I hazarded this conjecture, the father dismissed it abruptly. His daughter was crying and wringing her hands, repeating endlessly, "Alas! to die so young, to die unmarried!" The mother insulted me, calling me an infidel; she assured us that she, too, had seen the vampire with her own two eyes, and that she recognized him as Wiecznany. I resolved to keep quiet.

Every amulet in the house—and, indeed, in the village—was soon hung around Chava's neck, as her father swore to go disinter Wiecznany the next day and to burn him in the presence of all his relatives. In this manner the whole night went by; there was no calming them.

At daybreak, the entire village was stirring: the men were armed with rifles and daggers; the women carried red-hot horseshoes; the children had sticks and stones. We made our way to the cemetery, as shouts and insults were hurled at the deceased. With great effort, I emerged from the raging throng and went to stand beside the grave.

The exhumation took a long time. Everyone wanted to have a share in the effort, and so people were getting in one another's way; indeed, there would surely have been some accidents had the old men not given the order that only two men were to disinter the corpse itself. As soon as they removed the cloth that had covered the body, a frightfully high-pitched scream made my hair stand on end. The sound came from the woman beside me, who shouted, "It's a vampire! The worms have not eaten him!" All at once, a hundred mouths repeated her words, even as the corpse's head was being blown to pieces by twenty rifles shooting at point-blank range. Chava's father and relatives continued to assail the body with heavy blows of their long knives. Women used linens to soak up the red liquid that gushed from the mutilated body so it could be rubbed on the victim's neck.

Despite the riddled state of the corpse, several young men removed it from the grave and took the precaution of tying it securely to the trunk of a fir tree. With all the children following behind them, they dragged the body to a small orchard facing Poglonović's house. There, a heap of firewood and straw had been prepared in advance. They set fire to it, then threw the corpse on the pile and began to dance around it, each of the men shouting louder than his neighbor, as they continuously fanned the flames. The stench that emerged therefrom soon forced me to leave their company and return to my lodgings.

The house was filled with people; the men were smoking pipes, and the women were talking all at once and peppering the victim with questions, as she, still terribly pale, barely managed to reply. Wrapped around her neck were scraps of fabric saturated with the revolting red liquid that they took to be blood, which made for a ghastly contrast with poor Chava's bared shoulders and neck.

Little by little the crowd dispersed, until I was the only remaining visitor in the household. The illness was prolonged. Chava dreaded nightfall and wanted someone to watch over her at all times. Her parents, fatigued by their daily work, could scarcely keep their eyes open, so I offered my services as an overnight companion, which they gratefully accepted. I knew that, from a Morlachian perspective, there was nothing improper about my proposal.

I shall never forget the nights I spent at that unfortunate girl's bedside. She shuddered at every creak of the floor, at every whistle of the north wind, at the faintest of sounds. When she dozed off, she saw ghastly visions; all too often, she awoke with a start and screamed. Her imagination had been troubled by a dream, and now all the old busybodies in the countryside had managed to drive her mad with their frightening tales. She often said to me, as she felt her eyelids growing heavy, "Do not fall asleep, I beseech you. Hold a rosary in one hand and your dagger in the other; watch over me." On other occasions, she would not sleep unless she could hold my arm between her hands, clutching so tightly that the outline of her fingers was visible on my arm long afterward.

Nothing could distract her from the dismal thoughts that hounded her. She was terribly afraid of death, and she believed herself lost and helpless, despite all our efforts to console her. Within a matter of days, she had grown shockingly thin; all the color had drained from her lips, and her large, dark eyes looked glassy. Truly, she was a dreadful sight to behold.

I attempted to influence her imagination by pretending to see matters as she did. Alas, having initially mocked her credulity, I was no longer entitled to her trust. I told her that I had learned white magic in my country and knew a very powerful spell against evil spirits; if she wished, I said, I would take the risk upon myself and utter the spell, out of love for her.

At first, her inherent goodness made her fear the consequences for my soul. Before long, however, her fear of death overpowered her concern for me, and she bade me try the spell. I had committed a few passages of Racine to memory; I recited the French verses aloud before the poor girl, who believed she was hearing the devil's own tongue. Then, repeatedly rubbing her neck, I pretended to remove from it a small red agate that I had hidden between my fingers. I solemnly assured her that I had removed it from her neck and that she was saved. But she looked sadly at me and said, "You are lying; you had that stone in a little box. I saw you with it. You are no magician." Thus my ruse had done more harm than good. From that moment on, her condition did not cease to decline.

The night before her death, she said to me, "It is my own fault if I die. A boy from the village wanted to elope with me, but I refused. I told him I would go with him only if he gave me a silver chain. He went to Makarska to buy one, and while he was away, the vampire came. But if I hadn't been home," she added, "perhaps he would have killed my mother. So it is for the best." The next day she called for her father and made him promise to cut her throat and legs himself to keep her from becoming a vampire; she did not want anyone other than her father committing these useless atrocities upon her body. Then she kissed her mother and asked her to go and bless a rosary at the tomb of a man considered holy by the people of the village, and bring it back to her afterward. I admired the sensitivity shown by that country girl in finding such a pretext to prevent her mother from witnessing her last moments. She asked me to remove an amulet from around her neck. "Keep it," she said to me; "I hope it will be of more use to you than it was to me." Then, with great piety, she received the sacraments. Two or three hours later, her breathing grew heavy and her eyes grew still. Suddenly she grasped her father's arm and attempted to fling herself against his chest; and then she was dead. Her illness had lasted eleven days.

A few hours later, I left the village, vehemently condemning vampires, revenants, and all those who tell tales of such things.

Lovely Sofija[76]

An Opera in One Act

Characters:

NIKIFOROS
THE BEY OF MOJNO
A HERMIT
THE KUM[77]
SOFIJA
Choir of Young Men
Choir of the Svati[78]
Choir of Maidens

1

The Young Men

Young men of Vračina, saddle your black coursers, saddle them with their embroidered pads! Adorn yourselves this day with your newest finery. Every man must be well attired; every man must

---

76. This piece, which is very old and was written for the stage (a rarity in Illyrian poetry), is treated by Morlachian gusle players as a model of the form. The theme of this ballad is said to be based on a true story, as evidenced by an old gravesite in the Sinj Valley, the resting place of the lovely Sofija and the Bey of Mojno.

77. The *kum* is the godfather of either the bride or the groom. He accompanies them to the church and, later, into their bedroom, where he unties the groom's belt. (According to an old superstition, the groom must not cut, tie, or untie anything on his wedding day.) The kum even has the right to demand that the bride and groom be undressed in his presence. When he deems the marriage consummated, he fires a pistol once into the air, whereupon all the *svati* join in with cries of joy and gunfire.

78. These are the members of both families who have gathered for the wedding. The head of one family acts as the elder of the svati; he is called the *stari-svat*. Two young men, called *deveri*, accompany the bride until the *kum* places her in her husband's care.

bear his silver-handled yataghan and filigreed pistols on this day. For is this not the day when the wealthy Bey of Mojno is to marry the lovely Sofija?

2
Nikiforos

Mother, mother, has my black mare been saddled? Mother, mother, my black mare has neighed. Hand me the gilded pistols that I took from a binbashi. Hand me my yataghan with the silver hilt. Mother, listen to me: I still have ten sequins in a silken purse and I wish to throw them to the wedding musicians. For is this not the day when the wealthy Bey of Mojno is to marry the lovely Sofija?

3
The Svati

O Sofija, put on your red veil, for the procession is advancing; hearken to the sound of the pistols they are shooting in your honor.[79] Let the women sing us the tale of Ivan Valatiano and the lovely Agata. You, old men, let your gusles resound; and you, Sofija, take a sieve and throw some walnuts.[80] May you have as many sons as walnuts in your sieve! The wealthy Bey of Mojno is to marry the lovely Sofija.

---

79. During the bridal procession, the svati fire their pistols continually—this being an obligatory accompaniment to any celebration—as they howl and wail most dreadfully. Add to this the music of the old gusle players and the young ladies who sing epithalamia, often improvised, and you will have some idea of the abominable racket one hears at a Morlachian wedding.

80. When the bride arrives at the groom's home, she receives a sieve filled with nuts, given to her by her mother-in-law or another female relative of the groom. She throws the sieve over her head and then kisses the threshold.

4
Sofija

Walk at my right hand, mother; walk at my left hand, sister. Big brother, hold the horse by the bridle; little brother, hold onto the crupper. Ah! Who is that fair young man advancing on a black mare? Why is he not among the young svati? Ah! I see his face: it is Nikiforos. I fear that some misfortune shall come about. Nikiforos loved me long before the wealthy Bey of Mojno did.

5
Nikiforos

Sing, ladies! Sing like cicadas! I have but ten gold pieces; I shall give five of them to the singers and five to the gusle players. O Bey of Mojno, why do you look upon me with fear? Are you not the lovely Sofija's beloved? Do you not possess as many sequins as gray hairs in your beard? My pistols are not intended for you. Onward, black mare! Gallop to the Valley of Tears. Tonight I shall remove your saddle and bridle; tonight you shall be free and have no master.

6
The Maidens

Sofija, Sofija, may all the saints bless and keep you! Bey of Mojno, may all the saints bless and keep you! May you have a dozen handsome sons; may they be fair-haired, bold, and courageous! The sun is setting and the bey waits alone beneath his felted tent. Sofija, make haste! Bid your mother farewell and follow the kum. Tonight you shall lie on silken bedding, for you are the wife of the wealthy Bey of Mojno.

7

The Hermit

Who dares to fire a pistol so close to my cave? Who dares kill deer under the protection of Saint John Chrysostom and his hermit? Alas, it is not a deer that was hit; that bullet killed a man, and there is his black mare roaming free. May God have mercy upon your soul, poor traveler! I shall dig a grave in the sand near the stream.

8

Sofija

O my lord, how cold are your hands! O my lord, how damp is your hair! In spite of your Persian blankets, I am trembling in your bed. Truly, my lord, your body is glacial. I am cold, shivering, trembling; my limbs are covered in cold sweat. Alas! Holy mother of God, have mercy upon me, for I believe that I am like to die.

9

The Bey of Mojno

Where is she? Where is my beloved, the lovely Sofija? Why has she not joined me beneath my felted tent? Slaves, make haste to search for her, and tell the ladies to sing more intensely still; in the morning I will shower walnuts and gold pieces upon them. Let my mother bring the lovely Sofija back to the kum, for long have I waited alone beneath my tent.

10

The Kum

Noble svati, let each man fill his glass, and let each man empty his glass again! The bride has taken our sequins and stolen our silver chains.[81] By way of vengeance, we shan't leave a single pitcher of brandy in their home. The bride and groom have withdrawn and I have untied the groom's belt; let us then be joyful. The lovely Sofija has married the wealthy Bey of Mojno.

11
Sofija

What have I done to you, my lord, that you apply such pressure upon my chest? It feels as though a leaden corpse were on my breast. Holy mother of God, my throat is so tight that I do believe I shall suffocate. O friends, come to my aid, for the Bey of Mojno seeks to strangle me! Mother, mother, come to my aid, for he has bitten the vein in my neck and is sucking my blood!

---

81. A bride's dowry consists only of her clothing and, in some cases, a cow. However, she has the right to request a gift from each of the svati. Moreover, anything she can steal from them is fair game. I lost a handsome watch that way back in 1812; luckily, though, the bride had no idea how valuable it was, so I was able to buy it back from her in exchange for a few sequins.

VANJA

1

Vanja was to return to town, spending the night in a cemetery. But he was more lily-livered than a woman, and he shivered as though stricken with fever.

2

Once he was in the cemetery, he looked to his right and to his left, and he heard a sort of gnawing sound, which he took to be a vrykolaka feasting inside its tomb.[82]

3

"Alas," he cried, "I am done for! If it sees me, it will seek to eat me, fat as I am! I must eat some of the earth from its grave,[83] or else I am doomed."

4

And so he bent down to gather some earth; but a dog gnawing on a sheep bone, believing that Vanja sought to take it from him, leapt at his leg and bit him, drawing blood.

---

82. A type of vampire. (See the chapter "On Vampirism.")

83. Regarded as highly effective, this preventive measure is a widespread practice.

IMPROVISATION[84]

BY HIJACINT MAGLANOVIĆ

1

Stranger, what do you ask of the old gusle player? What do you want from old Maglanović? Have you not noticed the whiteness of his mustache, the trembling of his withered hands? How could this broken old man be expected to draw sound from his gusle, which is as old as he?

2

Long ago, Hijacint Maglanović had a black mustache and a steady hand for aiming a heavy pistol at its target. He was surrounded by young men and women, their mouths agape in admiration, at any celebration where he deigned to sit and draw music from his resonant gusle.

3

Shall I sing again, so that the young gusle players might smile and say amongst themselves, "Hijacint Maglanović is dead! His gusle is out of tune! That broken old man is rambling on! He ought to leave the honor of enchanting the nighttime hours, making the time pass more quickly with their singing, to those more skillful than he"?

---

84. I have every reason to believe that this piece truly was improvised. Maglanović was renowned among his countrymen for his impromptu performances, of which this is, according to local connoisseurs, among his finest.

4

May those young gusle players come forward, then, and may their harmonious verse be heard! Old Maglanović challenges them all. Just as he defeated their fathers in singing duels, so he shall defeat them all; for Hijacint Maglanović is like an old castle lying in ruin.[85] Do new houses possess the same beauty?

5

Hijacint Maglanović's gusle is as old as he, but it has never once disgraced itself by accompanying a mediocre tune. When the old poet is dead, who will dare draw a note from his gusle? No one: for as a warrior is buried with his saber, so too shall Maglanović rest in the earth with his gusle laid across his chest.

---

85. An allusion to the imposing ruins of ancient monuments, ubiquitous in these parts.

KONSTANTIN JAKOBOVIĆ

1

Konstantin Jakobović was sitting on a bench in front of his home. His child stood before him, playing with a saber; his wife Miljada was at his feet, cowering on the ground.[86] A stranger emerged from the forest and greeted him, taking him by the hand.

2

He had the face of a young man, yet his hair was white, his eyes doleful, his cheeks hollow, and his gait unsteady. "Brother," he said, "I am thirsty indeed, and I wish to drink." Miljada stood up at once and hastened to bring the man some brandy and milk.

3

"Brother, what distant hill is that, with trees so green?" — "Have you never been in these parts, then," asked Konstantin Jakobović, "that you recognize not the cemetery of our people?" — "Ah!" said the stranger. "It is there that I should like to have my resting place, for I feel that I am dying little by little."

4

He then took off his wide, red belt, revealing a bleeding gash in his chest. — "Yesterday I was shot by a heathen dog, and his bullet has torn through me; I can neither live nor die." Hearing this, Miljada

---

86. In a Morlachian household, the husband sleeps on a bed (if there is one in the house), while his wife sleeps on the floor. This provides yet more evidence of the disdain with which women are treated in that country. Indeed, a husband never mentions his wife's name in the presence of a stranger without adding: *Da prostite, moya xena* ("My wife, begging your pardon").

supported the man's body and Konstantin Jakobović probed his wound.

5

"Wretched, wretched was my life! So too shall be my death. But I wish to be buried atop that hillock, bathed in the light of the sun; for once I was a great warrior, before my hand came to find a saber too heavy to bear."

6

And with that, his mouth formed a smile, his eyes bulged out of their sockets, and his head abruptly tilted to one side. Miljada cried out, "O Konstantin, help me! This stranger is too heavy for me to bear his weight on my own." And Konstantin realized that the man was dead.

7

He loaded the body onto his horse and brought it to the cemetery, never stopping to consider whether the Catholic burial ground would suffer the presence of a Greek schismatic's corpse.[87] They dug a grave for him in a sunny spot and buried him with his saber and dagger, as befits a warrior.

8

When a week had passed, a dreadful pallor had come upon the lips of Konstantin's child, and the boy struggled even to walk. He lay lethargically on a mat, he who was so given to running about. But Providence brought to Konstantin's door a holy hermit, his neighbor.

---

87. A Greek buried in a Roman cemetery will become a vampire, and vice versa.

9

"Your child," he said, "has fallen victim to a most peculiar malady. Witness that red mark on his lily-white neck: the mark of a vampire's tooth." With that, the hermit put his books into a bag and made his way to the cemetery, where, at his request, the stranger's grave was opened.

10

The man's body was fresh as a daisy, his complexion pink as a rose. His beard had grown and his nails were as long as an eagle's talons; blood flowed from his mouth and flooded the grave. Konstantin picked up a stake to drive into the body, but the corpse let out a scream and fled into the woods.

11

Not even a horse spurred so violently as to bleed from its flanks could have run as fast as that monster did.[88] So forceful was he that saplings bent under his weight and great boughs snapped as though they had frozen.

12

The hermit, having gathered some blood and earth from the grave, rubbed it on the child's body; Konstantin and Miljada in turn did the same. That night, they said, "This was the hour at which the wicked stranger died." And just as they thus spoke, their dog wailed and hid between its master's legs.

---

88. Ottoman stirrups bear a resemblance to flat shoes, but have sharp edges; they therefore function as spurs.

13

The door opened and a giant entered, stooping as he came through the doorway. He sat down with his legs crossed, yet his head reached the beams of the house. Smiling, he stared at Konstantin, who, unable to look away, was entranced by the vampire.

14

But then the hermit opened his book. He tossed a sprig of rosemary onto the fire and blew the smoke toward the creature; then he cast him out in the name of Jesus. Soon the vampire trembled and dashed away through the door, like a wolf pursued by hunters.

15

The next day, at the very same hour, the dog wailed, the door opened, and a man came in and sat down. He had the stature of a soldier, and once more he set his gaze upon Konstantin in order to enchant him; but the hermit cast him out and he fled.

16

And the day after that, into the house came a dwarf so tiny that a rat might have made a fitting steed for him. And yet he had a lethal gaze, his eyes shining like two torches; but the hermit cast him out for a third time, and he fled forever.

Impromptu[89]

The snow at the summit of Mount Prologh is no whiter than your bosom. A cloudless sky is no bluer than your eyes. The shine of your gold necklace cannot compare to that of your golden locks, and a cygnet's down is no softer to the touch. When you open your mouth, it is as though I were looking upon blanched almonds. Ah, how fortunate is your husband! May you give him sons who resemble you!

---

89. This impromptu was performed, at my request, by an old Morlach for an English lady who was in Trogir in 1816.

In *Voyage d'Orenbourg à Boukhara*, by Colonel Baron Georges de Meyendorff, I found a remarkably similar song written by a Kyrgyz maiden. With permission, I include it here.

KYRGYZ SONG

Do you see that snow? My skin is whiter still. On that snow, do you see the blood of a slaughtered sheep? The red of my cheeks is deeper still. Go to that mountain and you will find a burnt tree trunk; my hair is blacker still.

At the sultan's palace, mullahs write in the blackest of ink; yet my eyebrows are darker still.

THE VAMPIRE[90]

1

In the marsh near Stăvila, a corpse lies on its back beside a spring. It is the body of that damned Venetian who deceived Maria and burned down our houses. A bullet pierced his throat and a yataghan was driven into his heart; and yet his blood has flowed, red and warm, for the three days he has lain on the ground.

2

His blue eyes are lifeless, yet they look to the sky. Woe to whomever should pass near that corpse, for who could help but fall under the spell of his gaze? His beard has grown, as have his nails.[91] The crows flee from him in terror, even as they seize upon the bodies of the brave hajduks strewn on the ground all around him.

3

His mouth is bloodied, yet it bears the smile of a man asleep, tormented by a most hideous love. Come, Maria, and behold the man for whom you betrayed family and country! Dare you kiss his pallid, blood-stained lips, which had such a talent for deception? He caused many tears to flow in his lifetime; in death he shall cause greater sorrow still.

....

---

90. This fragment of a ballad has little to recommend it other than its vivid description of a vampire. It appears to take as its subject some skirmish waged by the hajduks against the Venetian potestates.

91. Clear evidence of vampirism.

THE FEUD BETWEEN LEPA
AND CHERNYEGOR[92]

1

Cursed be Ostoix and cursed be Nicolò Ziani, he of the evil eye! May their wives be unfaithful and their children deformed! May they perish like the cowards they are! They caused the deaths of these two brave leaders.

2

Let those who are able to read and write, and those who like to sit idly about, spend their time selling fabric in town; but let any man with a sense of valor carry a saber at his side and go off to war, where young men acquire riches.

3

O Lepa! O Chernyegor! The wind is rising; unfurl now your sails. The Holy Virgin and Saint Eusebius are watching over your lithe vessels. They are like two eagles descending from the dark mountain to ravish the lambs on the plains.

---

92. Clearly, this riveting ballad has not come to us in its entirety. We believe that the piece we translate here was once part of a poem, only a single portion of which has survived, about the lives of the pirates Lepa and Chernyegor.

The first stanza inveighs against those responsible for the two heroes' deaths. Based on their names, one of the culprits whom the poet appears to accuse of treachery must have been Morlachian, while the other was Dalmatian or Italian.

The second stanza is written in a different meter than the first, and I am not sure whether the old man from whom I acquired the verse was right to include it with the rest of the ballad. In any case, the sentiments expressed therein are nearly universal among the Morlachs. It is not until the fourth stanza that the tale of the feud between the two friends actually begins.

4

Lepa is a brave warrior, and Chernyegor, too, is a brave soldier. They pilfer many valuables from wealthy, idle city folk, but they are generous toward gusle players, as the brave must rightly be: they give alms to the poor.[93]

5

That is how they won the hearts of the most beautiful of women. Lepa wedded the lovely Yevekhimia; Chernyegor wedded the fair Nastasia; and, whenever they returned from the sea, they called upon the services of skilled gusle players and made merry over glasses of wine and brandy.

6

Once, having seized a well-appointed barque, they towed it to the shore and discovered a lavish brocade gown within.[94] Its owner must have been sad indeed to lose such exquisite material; but the gown was to cause even greater sorrow, for Lepa coveted it, and Chernyegor did as well.

7

"I was the first to board this barque," said Lepa. "I want this gown for myself, to give to my wife, Yevekhimia." — "No," said Chernyegor, "take all the rest instead; I desire that my wife, Nastasia, be adorned with this gown." And so the two began to tug at the gown, all but tearing it to pieces.

---

93. Here, the author ingenuously reveals the basis for his admiration of the two bandits.

94. It is common knowledge that, in the past, Venice produced a great quantity of gold and silver brocade fabric destined for the Levant.

8

Chernyegor's face went white with rage. "Come hither, my young warriors," he cried, "and help me take this gown!" And with that, he drew his pistol; but the bullet missed Lepa, killing his page instead.[95] In an instant, their sabers were unsheathed. It was an awful thing to witness; so, too, is it awful to recount.

9

Finally, an aged gusle player rushed forward and cried, "Stop! Would you kill your brothers for a brocade gown?" Then he seized the gown and tore it to pieces.[96] Lepa was the first to sheathe his sword, and Chernyegor followed suit; but he looked askance at Lepa, because his side had suffered one loss more than had Lepa's.[97]

10

They did not shake hands, as was their custom; they went their separate ways, with anger in their hearts and vengeance on their minds. Lepa went off to the mountains; Chernyegor followed the coastline. Lepa said to himself, "He killed my beloved page, who used to light my pipe; he will pay the price for this.

11

"I will go to his house and abduct the wife he so adores; I will sell her to the Turks, and he shall never see her again." He set off with

---

95. Chiefs always have a page by their side. In peacetime, the page brings their pipe and prepares their coffee; in wartime, he loads their weapons. Such are the primary duties of a Morlachian page.

96. This act bespeaks the deference paid to poets and the elderly.

97. When a person has been murdered, the victim's family seeks to kill someone from the opposing clan. That death is avenged in turn, and so on and so forth; it is not unusual for twenty people or more to die in the course of a year over a feud in which they took no part. A respectable truce can be made only when each family has suffered an equal number of deaths; to reconcile when one's side has suffered an additional loss is to admit defeat.

a dozen men for Chernyegor's house. He did not find Chernyegor at home; soon I will tell you why.

12

When he arrived at Chernyegor's house, he beheld the fair Nastasia cooking lamb.[98] "Good day, my lord," said she. "Will you have a glass of brandy?" — "I am not here to drink brandy," he said; "I am here to carry you away with me. You will be a slave, and you shall never be ransomed."

13

He seized fair Nastasia and, despite her pleas, took her away in his barque and went to sell her to a caravel anchored near the shore. I now shall cease my singing of Lepa to sing of Chernyegor instead. He was furious about having one loss more than did Lepa. "Cursed be my hand, which missed its target: my deceitful enemy!

14

"Since I cannot kill him, I shall kidnap his beloved wife and sell her to that caravel anchored near the shore. When he returns home, never again to see his Yevekhimia, he will surely die of sorrow." And so, with his rifle strapped to his back, he approached the home of lovely Yevekhimia.

15

"Arise, Yevekhimia! arise, wife of Lepa! You must follow me down to that ship." — "How can this be, my lord?" she cried. "Would you betray your brother?" Showing her no mercy, he seized her by her dark hair and carried her on her shoulders, first to his barque, then on board the caravel.

---

98. Literally: seasoned, smoked mutton with cabbage, a dish the Illyrians call *paçterma*.

16

"Captain, I want six hundred gold pieces for this woman." — "That is too much," said the captain. "I just bought another woman, more beautiful still, for five hundred." — "Give me five hundred gold pieces, then," replied Chernyegor, "but show that woman to me." And so, receiving five hundred gold pieces, he handed over the lovely Yevekhimia as she wept.

17

They entered the cabin and the captain lifted fair Nastasia's veil. When Chernyegor recognized his beloved wife, he cried out and, for the first time, tears flowed from his dark eyes. He attempted to ransom his wife, but the Turk refused to sell her.

18

With clenched fists, he leapt back onto his barque. "Row, young men, row to the shore! All my warriors must join together to take that great ship, for my beloved Nastasia is held captive within." As foam washed over the bow, the barque glided over the water like a wild duck.

19

As he approached the shore, he beheld Lepa, who was pulling his hair out. "Alas! Yevekhimia, my wife, you are a prisoner in that caravel; I shall rescue you or die in the attempt!" Chernyegor leapt to the ground, walked right up to Lepa, and shook his hand.

20

"I kidnapped your wife and you kidnapped mine; I killed your beloved page and you killed one more of my men. Let us be quits;

let our hatred perish. Let us be united, as once we were, and go together to take back our wives." Lepa shook his hand and said, "You speak well, brother."[99]

21

They called upon their young sailors, loaded their vessel with rifles and pistols, then rowed out to the caravel, brothers once again. What a beautiful sight it was to behold! They boarded that great ship. "Our women," they cried, "or you die!" They took back their wives, but neglected to pay the ransom.[100]

---

99. Here, *brother* is used as a synonym for *friend*.

100. This last detail is a typical characteristic.

LOVER IN A BOTTLE

1

All you young ladies who listen to me while braiding your hair, you would be fortunate indeed if you, like the lovely Chava,[101] could hide your lovers in a bottle.

2

A great wonder arose in the city of Trebinje: a young lady, the most beautiful of all her companions, refused all those who would court her, though they be young and fearless, handsome and wealthy.

3

But around her neck she wore a silver chain with a glass vial pendant, which she kissed and spoke to all the day long, calling it her beloved.

4

Her three sisters married three daring and powerful beys. "When shall you marry, Chava? Shall you ignore the young men until you have grown old?"

5

"I shall not marry," Chava said, "if I am to be merely a bey's wife, for I have a friend more powerful than any bey. If I desire some precious item, he brings it to me at my command.

---

101. Name equivalent to Eve.

6

"If I wish for a pearl from the bottom of the sea, he will dive to the seabed and bring it to me. Neither water nor earth nor fire can stop him when I have given my command.

7

"I have no fear of his infidelity; for there is no home—neither a felt tent nor a dwelling made of wood or stone—as enclosed as a glass bottle."

8

From all around Trebinje, people flocked to witness this prodigy; and indeed, if she asked for a pearl, a pearl was brought to her.

9

Should she wish for sequins to put in her hair,[102] she simply held out her skirt, and great handfuls of them collected there. Had she demanded the ducal crown, it would have been hers.

10

When the bishop learned of this wonder, it irked him. Seeking to drive out the demon, the object of lovely Chava's obsession, he saw to it that her precious bottle was wrested from her.

---

102. The women let their braided hair fall around their shoulders and adorn it with sequins. This fashion is particularly common in the districts bordering the Turkish provinces.

11

"Let all Christians join with me in prayer to drive out this black demon!" With that, he made the sign of the cross, took up a hammer, and struck the glass vial with a great blow.

12

The vial broke and blood spurted out of it. The lovely Chava cried out and dropped dead. It is a pity indeed that such a great beauty thus fell victim to a demon.[103]

---

103. In *The World Bewitched*, by the celebrated doctor Balthasar Bekker, I read a story with considerable similarities to this one:

"Around the year 1597, God answered the prayers of the faithful, revealing a particular spirit—the nature of which, dark or light, was not at first apparent—that caused many people to apostatize. There was a girl named Bietka who was sought after by a young man named Zachariasz. Both were natives of Wieclam, where they had been raised. And this young man, despite being a clergyman with aspirations of priesthood, ceased not his attentions and his promises of marriage. But his father turned him away from his plan by reminding him of the rank he held in the church. Seeing that his intentions toward the girl would be for naught, he gave himself over to such a profound melancholy that he took his own life, strangling himself. Not long after his death, a spirit appeared to that young girl, claiming to be the soul of that same Zachariasz who had hanged himself. The spirit told her he had been sent by God as a sign of His displeasure at this offense, and that he had come to wed her—she being the primary cause of his death—in fulfillment of his promise. That clever spirit coaxed the poor thing with promises of riches, convincing her that he was the soul of her dead beau, and so she agreed to marry him. Word of Bietka's impending nuptials with the spirit of Zachariasz spread ever more with each passing day, reaching throughout Poland, and crowds of the curious gathered from all directions.

"Some of the nobles gave credence to the spirit's words and met with him; some even welcomed him to their homes. In that way, Bietka amassed a great sum of money; for the spirit was willing to speak, to answer, to tell the future, but only with her consent. He spent a full year in the home of one Mr. Trepka, a steward from Krakow. From there, he went from house to house, finally settling in the home of a widow by the name of Wlodkow. There, over the course of two years' residence, the spirit tried out all his skills and played every trick he knew.

"These are the most significant thereof. He gave assurance of events past and present. He was an adept proponent of the Roman faith, going so far as to declaim against the Protestants, all of whom were, he asserted, damned. He wanted no Protestants to approach him, for he deemed them unworthy to speak to him, but he made exceptions for those who were, he was persuaded, more interested in novelty than in religion; and he turned some number of them back to popery. No one would have discovered that this spirit was the Devil had not some Poles traveled to Italy in the Jubilee Year of 1600 and spread word of the spirit of Zachariasz among the people there. A certain Italian who practiced the magical arts came to hear of this, some five years after the escape of that spirit from his imprisonment. He went to Poland to seek out the Wlodkow woman and, to the great astonishment of all those present, demanded restitution of the demon that had fled from him. The good woman having granted his request, he trapped the cunning spirit in a ring and returned it to Italy. According to the Italian, that demon would have caused terrible harm in Poland had he left it there."

KARIM-ALI, VAMPIRE

1

Karim-Ali crossed the yellow river,[104] then continued to the home of Vasilj Kaimis, where he stayed as a guest.

2

Vasilj Kaimis had a beautiful wife by the name of Jumelija, who fell in love when first she gazed upon Karim-Ali.

3

Karim-Ali was swathed in luxuriant furs and carried gilded pistols, but Vasilj was poor.

4

Jumelija was seduced by his wealth; indeed, what woman could resist such quantities of gold?

5

Having had his way with the faithless wife, Karim-Ali sought to bring her home with him to the land of the infidels.

6

And Jumelija said she would follow him. What an ignoble woman, choosing an infidel's harem over the conjugal bed!

---

104. Most likely the Zrmanja, which has a notable yellow tinge in autumn.

7

Karim-Ali picked her up by her slim waist and placed her in front of him atop his handsome steed, white as a November snow.

8

Where art thou, Vasilj? Karim-Ali, whom you took into your home, is abducting your beloved wife, Jumelija!

9

Vasilj ran along the banks of the yellow river and spotted the two traitors as they crossed it upon a white horse.

10

He picked up his long rifle bedecked with ivory and red crests.[105] He fired, and in the next instant, Karim-Ali was staggering upon his mount.

11

"Jumelija, Jumelija!" Karim-Ali cried. "Your love has cost me dearly. That filthy infidel has killed me, and he will kill you as well.

12

"I will give you a precious talisman with which you will buy his mercy, that he might spare your life.

---

105. This is a frequent decoration on rifles owned by the Illyrians and the Turks.

13

"Take this Koran, in its pouch of gilded red leather.[106] Whosoever consults it shall be wealthy and beloved of women.

14

"Whosoever carries this book, let him open it to the sixty-sixth page, and he shall command all the spirits on land and in the seas."

15

With that, he fell into the yellow river. His body floated there, leaving a cloud of red in the water.

16

Vasilj Kaimis ran to seize the horse by the bridle and raised his arm to strike his wife down.

17

"Grant me my life, Vasilj," she said, "and I shall give you a precious talisman whose bearer shall be wealthy and beloved of women.

18

"Whosoever carries this book, let him open it to the sixty-sixth page,[107] and he shall command all the spirits on land and in the seas."

---

106. Nearly all Muslims carry a Koran in a small pouch made of red leather.

107. The number sixty-six is said to be very powerful in spells.

19

Vasilj pardoned his faithless wife and accepted the book, which any Christian ought to throw into the fire in horror.

20

Night fell, a great wind picked up, and the yellow river overflowed, depositing the corpse of Karim-Ali on the shore.

21

When Vasilj opened the unholy book to the sixty-sixth page, the earth began to shake and split open with a dreadful noise.

22

A bloodied specter pierced through the ground. It was Karim-Ali. "Vasilj," he said, "now that you have renounced your God, you belong to me."

23

He grabbed the unhappy wretch and bit the vein in his neck, not releasing him until all his veins had dried up.

24

This story was told by Nikola Kostović, who heard it from Jumelija's grandmother.

POBRATIMI[108]

1

Ivan Lubović was born in Trogir. On one occasion, he went to the mountain town of Vrgorac, where he was an honored guest for eight days in the home of Kiril Zborić.

2

And Kiril Zborić went to Trogir and stayed at the home of Ivan Lubović, and for eight days they drank wine and brandy from the same cup.

3

When Kiril Zborić decided to return to his region, Ivan Lubović took him by the arm and said, "Let us go before a priest and be pobratimi."

4

And so they went before a priest, who said the holy prayers. They took communion together and swore to be brothers until one of the two should die.

---

108. This word is explained in the footnotes to "The Flame of Perušić."

5

One day, Ivan was sitting in front of his home, cross-legged,[109] smoking his pipe, when a young man with dust-covered feet appeared before him and greeted him.

6

"Ivan Lubović, I am sent by your brother Kiril Zborić. Near the mountain there is a godless dog who means him harm, and he asks that you help him defeat the infidel."

7

Ivan Lubović took up his rifle, put a shoulder of lamb in his bag, shut the door, and set out for Vrgorac.[110]

8

And the bullets those two pobratimi shot always struck their enemies in the heart; no man, however strong or nimble, would have dared to face them.

9

Thus it was that they took nanny goats and kids, valuable firearms, luxuriant fabrics, and silver coins, and they also took a beautiful Turkish woman.

---

109. This is the most common seated posture.

110. A Morlach's preparations for war are quite thoroughly detailed in these few words.

10

The goats, weapons, and cloth were divided equally, with Ivan Lubović taking one half and Kiril Zborić the other; but they could not divide the woman.

11

And they both wished to take her back to their own country, and they both loved her; and thus they quarreled for the first time in their lives.

12

But Ivan Lubović said, "We drank brandy and we know not what we do. Let us discuss this matter peacefully in the morning." With that, they lay down on the same mat and slept until morning.

13

Kiril Zborić was the first to awake, and he nudged Ivan Lubović to arise. "Now that you are sober," he said, "will you give me that woman?" But Ivan Lubović made no reply. He sat down and let tears flow from his dark eyes.

14

And so Kiril sat by his side. His gaze settled at times on the Turkish slave woman, at times on his friend, and occasionally at the khanjar hanging from his belt.

15

The young men who had accompanied them into battle wondered among themselves, "What will happen? Will these pobratimi break the bond of friendship they pledged to one another in church?"

16

When the two men had been sitting for a long time, they both rose to their feet. Ivan Lubović took the slave by her right hand; Kiril Zborić took her by her left hand.

17

And thus flowed from their eyes tears as heavy as raindrops in a summer storm. All of a sudden, they drew their khanjars and drove them into the slave's chest.

18

"Let the infidel perish, that our friendship may abide!" With that, they shook hands, and their love for one another never ceased.

This beautiful song was sung by the young gusle player Stjepan Špilja.

HADAGNY[111]

PART THE FIRST

1

Serral was at war with Ostrowicz. Swords had been drawn; six times had the earth swallowed the blood of the brave. Many a widow had dried her tears; more than one mother was weeping still.

2

On the mountain and in the plain, Serral and Ostrowicz had fought like rutting stags. Blood had been spilled from the hearts of both tribes, yet their hatred had not subsided.

3

One of Serral's esteemed old leaders beckoned his daughter and said, "Helena, go to Ostrowicz and see what our enemies are doing in the village there. I wish to end this war, which has lasted for six moons."

4

Helena put on her hat with the silver braiding and her good coat, red and embroidered,[112] and on her feet she wore strong shoes

---

111. This song is popular in Montenegro, or so I am told. It was on the banks of the Naretva that I heard it first.

112. In Montenegro, women serve as spies, yet they are respected by those whose forces they observe and who are aware of their mission. Even the slightest affront to a woman from an enemy tribe would be cause for eternal dishonor.

made from bison leather.[113] She set out for the mountain just as the sun was setting.

5

Ostrowicz's beys were seated around a fire. Some were polishing their weapons, and others were making cartridges. On a bundle of hay sat a gusle player, bringing pleasure to their vigil.

6

Hadagny, the youngest among them, turned his gaze toward the plain. He spotted someone approaching the mountain to spy on their camp. He jumped to his feet and grabbed a long rifle embellished with silver.

7

"Comrades," he said, "do you see that enemy creeping in the shadows? Had the light of our fire not been reflected on his hat,[114] we would have been caught unawares! But, so long as my rifle does not fail, he shall perish."

8

When he aimed his long rifle downward, he released the trigger, and the sound of the shot echoed through the valley. But another sound, yet more intense, was to be heard. Old Bietko, his father, cried out: "That is the voice of a woman!"

---

113. In Illyrian, *opanci*: a coarse leather sole tied to the leg with strips of cloth; the top of the foot is covered with a multicolored knit cloth. This shoe is worn by women and girls, and even in wealthy families, girls wear opanci until they are married. Once they are wed, if they so desire, they may wear *pashmak*, the fine leather slippers worn by Turkish women.

114. These hats are embellished with shiny medallions and stripes.

9

"Woe upon us!" the men cried. "Shame upon our tribe! He killed not a man armed with a rifle and a yataghan, but a woman!" And each of them took up a torch to get a better look.

10

They beheld the lifeless body of the lovely Helena, and their faces were tinged with red. Hadagny cried out, "For shame! I have killed a woman! Woe betide me! I have killed the one I loved!"

11

Bietko looked ominously at him. "You have dishonored our tribe, Hadagny. You must flee the country. What will Serral do when he learns that we kill women, as those hajduk thieves would do?"[115]

12

Hadagny sighed and turned for one last look at his father's house. Then he strapped his long rifle to his shoulder and descended the mountain to seek shelter in far-off lands.

13

This song was written by Ivan Višnjić, the most skillful of gusle players. Let those who wish to hear the further adventures of Hadagny pay the gusle player for his fine work.

---

115. The term *hajduk* is practically a curse word among the residents of wealthy villages.

Part the Second[116]

1

I was guarding my goats, leaning against my long rifle.[117] My dog was sleeping in the shade, and the cicadas were singing heartily on every blade of grass, for it was a day of abundant heat.

2

I saw a handsome young man emerge from the mountain pass. His clothing was tattered, yet brilliant embroidery was still visible beneath the rags. He carried a long rifle embellished with silver, and a yataghan hung from his belt.

3

He approached and greeted me, asking, "Brother, is this not the land of Ostrowicz?" I could not hold back my tears, and I heaved a great sigh. "Yes," I replied.

4

And then he said, "Ostrowicz was wealthy long ago; his flocks grazed all over the mountain and his warriors' rifles, gleaming in the sun, were four hundred in number. But now I see only you and a handful of mangy goats."

---

116. It is believed that this second part was written by a different author.

117. Men never leave their homes unarmed.

5

And I told him, "Ostrowicz was powerful, but great shame fell upon him and brought him misfortune. Serral vanquished him in battle after young Hadagny killed the lovely Helena."

6

"Tell me, brother," he said, "how it happened." — "Serral came down like a torrent. He killed our warriors, destroyed our crops, and sold our children to the infidels. Our days of glory have passed!"

7

"And what of old Bietko?" he asked. "Can you tell me of his fate?" — "When he saw his tribe in ruins, he climbed upon that boulder and called for his son Hadagny, who had set out for far-off lands.

8

"One of Serral's beys—all the saints damn him!—shot him with his rifle and slashed his throat with his yataghan; then, he kicked old Bietko so that he rolled into the chasm."

9

With that, the stranger fell facedown on the ground and, like an injured chamois, he rolled into the chasm where his father had fallen; for that stranger was Hadagny, son of Bietko, he who had caused our misfortune.

THE MONTENEGRINS[118]

1

Napoleon said, "Who are these men who dare to resist me? Let them throw their pistols and their niello-inlaid yataghans at my feet."[119] And with that, he sent twenty thousand soldiers to the mountain.

2

There were dragoons, infantrymen, cannons, and mortars. "Come to the mountain, where you will see five hundred brave Montenegrins. For their cannons, there are chasms; for their dragoons, there are boulders; and for their infantrymen, five hundred fine rifles."

3[120]

....

4

They set out, their weapons gleaming in the sunlight. They climbed the mountain in formation to burn down our villages, to seize our

---

118. Every minor population is convinced that the eyes of the world are upon it. Moreover, I am quite certain that Napoleon never took much heed of the Montenegrins.

119. This type of decoration is found on the handles of the most valuable weapons, especially yataghans. The hollows are filled with a lovely, bluish-black mixture, the secret to which is, it is said, lost in the Levant.

120. Here a stanza is missing.

women and children and take them back to their country.[121] When they got as far as the gray rock, they lifted their eyes and saw our red hats.

5

Then said their captain, "Let every man aim his rifle; let every man kill a Montenegrin." With that, they fired, striking down the red hats we had propped on stakes.[122] But we, lying on our stomachs behind those stakes, keenly returned fire.

6

"Hark! It is the echo of our rifles," said the captain. But before he could turn around, he fell down dead, as did twenty-five of his men. The others fled, and for all their lives, never did they dare set their gaze upon a red hat.

He who sang this song was at the gray rock with his brothers. His name is Gunther Vučirić.

---

121. Being accustomed to fighting with the Turks led the Montenegrins to assume that all nations committed similar atrocities during their military expeditions.

122. This ruse was employed frequently, with success.

Stjepan Tomašević and His Horse

Why do you weep, my fine white steed? Why do you sorrowfully neigh? Have you not the finest of harnesses? Are you not shod with silver, and with nails made of gold? Haven't you silver bells around your neck? Is not your master the King of fertile Bosnia? — I weep, master, for the infidel will strip the silver shoes and the golden nails from me, and my silver bells as well. And I neigh, master, because from the skin of the King of Bosnia, the infidel shall make for me a saddle.

THE MAGIC RIFLE

Whosoever should come to see the great bey Savić's rifle would behold a wonder. It has twelve barrel bands of gold and twelve of silver; the stock is inlaid with mother-of-pearl, and three red silk crests hang down from the trigger.

There are other rifles with gold barrel bands and red silk crests, and the gunsmiths in Banja Luka are skilled with mother-of-pearl. But where is the craftsman capable of casting the spell that makes every bullet from Savić's rifle deadly?

He fought the Hindu with his three-layered chainmail tunic, and he fought the Arnaut with his felt tabard lined with seven layers of silk. The chainmail was struck down like a spider's web, the tabard torn like a leaf from a plane tree.

Davud, the handsomest of the Bosnians, strapped the finest of his rifles to his back, filled his belt with sequins, and selected the most resonant of his dozen gusles. He left Banja Luka on Friday, and on Sunday he arrived in the land of the great bey Savić.

He sat and played a prelude on his gusle, and all the maidens gathered around him. When he played plaintive songs, all the maidens sighed; and when he played songs of love, the bey's daughter Nastasija threw her bouquet to him. Her cheeks red with shame, she fled into her house.

And that night she opened her window and saw Davud sitting on a stone bench near the door to her house. As she leaned down to look upon him, her red hat fell from her head, and Davud picked it up. When he returned it to the lovely Nastasija, it was filled with sequins.

"See there," he said, "that great cloud coming from the mountain, filled with rain and hail; would you leave me to die in front of you, exposed to the storm?" She removed her silk belt and tied one end of it to her balcony, and in an instant, the handsome Davud was by her side.

"Speak softly!" she said. "If my father were to hear us, he would kill us both." And so they spoke softly; and before long, they ceased to speak at all. The handsome Davud descended from the balcony sooner than Nastasija would have liked; but dawn was approaching, and he ran to the mountain to hide.

And every night, he returned to the village; and every night, the silk belt hung from the balcony. He stayed with his lover all night, but when the rooster crowed, he went to the mountain to hide. On the fifth night, he arrived bloodied and pale.

"Some hajduks attacked me," he said. "They were waiting for me at the mountain pass; when day breaks and I must leave you, they will kill me. And so I kiss you now for the last time. But if I had your father's magic rifle, who would dare lie in wait for me? Who would dare meet me in battle?"

"My father's rifle? But how could I give it to you? By day it is strapped to his back; by night he keeps it in his bed. If he found it gone in the morning, he would assuredly cut off my head." And so she cried, and looked to the eastern sky.

"Bring me your father's rifle and leave mine in its place; he will see no difference. My rifle has twelve barrel bands of gold and twelve of silver; the stock is inlaid with mother-of-pearl, and three red silk crests hang down from the trigger."

She entered her father's bedroom on tiptoe, holding her breath; she took his rifle and left Davud's in its place. The bey sighed in his sleep and cried out, "Jesus!" But he did not awake, and his daughter gave the magic rifle to the handsome Davud.

And Davud examined the rifle from stock to sight, inspecting the trigger, the flint, and the lock. He kissed Nastasija tenderly and swore he would return the next day.

He left her on Friday, and on Sunday he arrived in Banja Luka.

And the bey Savić was handling Davud's rifle. "I must be getting old," he said, "for my rifle feels heavy. But it still has many infidels left to kill." And every night, Nastasija's belt hung from her balcony, but the deceitful Davud did not appear.

The circumcised dogs came into our land, and no one could battle their leader, Davud-Aga. Slaves filled his leather bag with the ears of those he slaughtered. All the men of Varaždin gathered around the old bey Savić.

And Nastasija climbed atop the roof of her house to watch the vicious battle, and she recognized Davud as he spurred on his horse to charge at her elderly father. The bey, certain he could not miss, shot first, but the fuse alone caught fire, and the bey trembled in fear.

And Davud's bullet struck Savić beneath his armor, entering through his chest and exiting through his back. The bey heaved a sigh and fell dead. Then his head was cut off by a black man and hung by his white mustache from the tree of Davud's saddle.

When Nastasija saw her father's head, she did not weep or sigh. She dressed in her young brother's clothing, mounted her young brother's black horse, and rode through the melee, searching for Davud, to kill him. And when Davud saw that young horseman, he aimed the magic rifle at him.

And the bullet he shot was fatal. The lovely Nastasija heaved a sigh and fell dead. Then her head was cut off by a black man. But she had no mustache, so he removed her hat and held her head by her long hair; and Davud recognized the tresses as those of the lovely Nastasija.

And he leapt to the ground to kiss that bloodied head. "I would give a sequin," he cried, "for every drop of the lovely Nastasija's blood! I would give my arm to bring her, alive, to Banja Luka!" And he threw the magic rifle into the Varaždin well.

hundreds [illegible] and every [illegible] Natasha's [illegible] long [illegible] balcony [illegible] did not appear.

The crowd [illegible] in loud [illegible] could [illegible] Dave [illegible] Ellen [illegible] slaughtered [illegible] of V[illegible] [illegible]

[illegible] Natasha [illegible] stop [illegible] her [illegible] [illegible] the [illegible] [illegible] her [illegible] [illegible] [illegible]

[illegible] high [illegible] head [illegible] black [illegible] [illegible] the [illegible]

W[illegible] Natasha [illegible] her [illegible] [illegible] D[illegible] [illegible] [illegible]

And [illegible] her [illegible] [illegible] [illegible] her [illegible] lovely N[illegible]

And [illegible] [illegible] [illegible] [illegible] Viva [illegible]!

THE BAN OF CROATIA

Once there was a Ban of Croatia who was blind in the right eye and deaf in the left ear. With his right eye he beheld the misery of the people, and with his left ear he listened to the grievances of the voivodes; and whosoever possessed great wealth was accused, and whosoever was accused died. Thus he had the bey Humanay decapitated, and the voivode Zambolić likewise, and he seized their treasures. But God came to lose patience with his crimes and allowed his specters to trouble the man's sleep. And every night, Humanay and Zambolić stood at the foot of his bed, staring at him with their dull, mournful eyes. And every morning, when the stars faded and the sky grew pink in the east, a dreadful thing occurred. The two specters bent as if to bow in greeting, mocking him; and their heads, having no support, fell and rolled on the rug. And only then could the Ban fall asleep. One night—a cold winter night—Humanay spoke, saying, "Long have we bowed to you. Why do you not return our greeting?" And so the Ban arose, trembling. And as he bowed before them, his head fell from his body and rolled across the rug.

THE DYING HAJDUK

"Come to me, old white eagle! It is I, Gabrijel Salopek, who so often fed you the flesh of my enemies the pandours. I am wounded; I am dying. But before you give my great heart to your eaglets, I ask that you do one thing for me. Take my empty cartridge box to my brother Đurađ, that he might avenge me. In my box there were twelve cartridges, and you will find twelve dead pandours all around me. But the pandours were thirteen in number, and the thirteenth of them was Božić, the coward who struck me in the back. Take also this embroidered handkerchief in your talons and bring it to the lovely Chava, that she might mourn me." And the eagle carried his empty cartridge box to his brother Đurađ, and found him drunk on brandy; and he carried the embroidered handkerchief to the lovely Chava, and found her being married to Božić.[123]

---

123. Last year, while in Athens, I read a Greek poem whose ending is analogous to that of this ballad. Great minds do think alike. Here is a translation thereof.

THE MAIDEN IN HADES

Happy the mountains, well apportioned the fields, they who know not Charon, who await not Charon! In summer the sheep, in winter the snows. — Three gallant young men wish to leave Hades. One says he will leave in the month of May, the second in summer, the third in autumn when the grapes are ripe. — A fair maiden speaks to them in the underworld, saying, "Take me with you, gallant young men! Bring me where there is air, where there is light." — "Little girl," they said, "your skirts rustle, the wind whistles through your hair, and your slippers are coming undone; Charon would hear." — "Then I shall remove my skirt, cut my hair, and leave my little slippers at the bottom of the stairs. But take me with you, gallant young men! Take me to the world above, that I might see my mother who mourns for me, my brothers who weep for me." — "Little girl, those brothers of yours are dancing at a ball," they said. "Little girl, that mother of yours is prating in the street."

"Come ... our white eagle ... [illegible] ... gotten red on the neck of my enemies ... [illegible] ... ask that you do one thing for me. Take my copper ... to my brother ... that he ... [illegible] ... were twelve ... all around me ... the thirteenth ... [illegible] ... the ... [illegible] ... and brought ... [illegible] ... and found ... [illegible] ... hand ... [illegible] ... Red.

[illegible]

[illegible]

MOURNING SONG
OF THE NOBLE WIFE OF HASAN-AGA[124]

What are those patches of white on the verdant hills? Snow, perhaps, or swans? Were there snow, it would have melted. Were there swans, they would have taken flight. Those patches are neither snow nor swans, but the tents of Hasan-Aga. He bemoans his agonizing wounds. His mother and his sister have come to heal him, but his beloved wife, inhibited by timidity, is not by his side.[125]

When the pain had subsided, he had a message given to his loyal wife: "Do not look upon me in my white house, nor before my people." Hearing these words, the lady withdrew to her apartment, afflicted with sorrow. Then, the sound of horses' hooves resounded near the house, and the poor wife of Hasan-Aga, believing her husband to be near, ran to her balcony. But her two daughters followed close behind her and cried, "Stop, dear mother! That is not our father, Hasan-Aga; it is our uncle, Pintorović-Bey."

The ill-fated woman stopped and held her beloved brother in her arms. "Such shame, my brother!" she cried. "He is repudiating me, when I have given him five children!"

---

124. The esteemed Abbe Fortis famously translated this lovely ballad in Italian verse. I have no pretension of translating it as well as he, but I have translated it differently; the sole merit of my translation is its literality.

The setting is in Bosnia and the characters are Muslim, as evidenced by the words *aga*, *kadi*, etc.

125. We may find it difficult to understand how timidity would prevent a good wife from tending to her convalescent husband. However, Hasan-Aga's wife is Muslim, and according to her notions of decency, she must never appear before her husband without being called. Hasan-Aga, however, found it irritating, which suggests that her modesty is excessive. The two verses in Illyrian are remarkably concise, a quality that makes them rather obscure:

> *Oblaziga mater i sestriza;*
> *A gliubovza od stida ne mogla.*
> Came the mother and came the sister,
> But the beloved, out of shame, could not.

The bey gravely held his tongue and pulled from a red silk purse a piece of paper that set her free.[126] Now she will be able to wear a bridal crown again, once she has returned to her mother's home.

The lady, having read this document, kissed her two sons on the forehead and her two daughters on their ruby lips; but she could not tear herself from her youngest, still in the cradle. Her merciless brother wrested her (with some difficulty) away from her child, placed her atop his horse, and returned with her to their parents' white house. She did not remain there long. High-born and beautiful, she was soon sought after by the noblemen of the country. Among these, the Kadi of Imotski stood out.

The lady pleaded, "Brother, would that you should outlive me! Do not give me to any man, I beseech you.[127] My heart would break were I to see my children orphaned." Ali-Bey took no heed of her words, but committed her to the Kadi of Imotski.

She appealed to him one last time, asking that a message be sent to the Kadi of Imotski: "Greetings from the young lady, who wishes to convey a request. When you arrive with the esteemed svati, bring a long veil to cover your fiancée from head to foot so that, when she passes before the Aga's house, she will not see her orphans."

When the Kadi had read that letter, he gathered his esteemed svati. The svati went to collect the bride from her home. They were joyful when they left with her.

When they passed before the Aga's house, her two daughters recognized their mother from atop the balcony, and her two sons ran out to meet her, calling, "Stop, mother dear! Come have tea with us!" The unfortunate mother cried out to the stari-svat, "For

---

126. *Knigu oprochienja*. Literally, a freedom paper; a divorce decree.

127. As the head of the family, Pintorović-Bey has the right to dispose of his sister as he would a horse or a piece of furniture.

This ballad is notable for the delicacy of the sentiments expressed therein. Abbe Fortis published the original alongside his translation—or, rather, an imitation in Italian verse. I believe my version to be a precise and literal translation, as my work was overseen by a Russian, who gave me the meaning word by word.

Mr. Charles Nodier has also published a translation of this ballad, following his delightful poem *Smarra*.

the love of God, brother stari-svat, stop the horses near that house, that I might give something to my orphans." The horses stopped near the house, and she gave gifts to her children. To her two sons, she gave shoes embroidered in gold; to her daughters, brightly colored dresses; and for the little one, still in the cradle, she sent a lightweight gown.

Hasan-Aga watched from a distance and called to his two sons, "Come to me, my orphans; leave that heartless mother who has abandoned you!"

At that, the poor mother grew pale. Her head struck the floor and in that moment, the pain of seeing her orphaned children caused her to cease living.

Miloš Kobilić[128]

How beautiful are the red roses in Lazar's white palace! Who could say which of them is the most beautiful, the pinkest, the grandest?

For these are not roses at all, but the young daughters of Lazar, he who rules over the vast plains of Serbia, a hero and a prince, the heir to an ancient lineage.

Lazar married his daughters off to nobles: Vukasava to Miloš Kobilić,[129] Mara to Vuk Branković, and Milica to Sultan Bayezid.[130] Then he married Jelena to the noble lord Đurađ Stracimirović, the young voivode from Zeta.[131]

After some time had passed, three of the sisters visited their mother. But the Sultana Milica did not join them, for Bayezid forbade it. The young sisters greeted one another kindly, but alas, before long they were quarreling in Lazar's white palace, each one boasting of her husband.

Lady Jelena, wife of Đurađ Stracimirović, said, "No mother has ever birthed a knight as noble and brave as did the mother of Đurađ Stracimirović."

Branković's wife said, "No mother has ever birthed a knight as noble and brave as did the mother of Vuk Branković."

---

128. I owe the ballad which follows to the kindness of the late Count of Sorgo, who found the Serbian original in a manuscript at the Arsenal Library in Paris. He believed this poem to have been composed by a contemporary of the eponymous Miloš.

The quarrel among Lazar's daughters, the duel between two of his sons-in-law, the betrayal of Vuk Branković, and Miloš's devotion are conveyed herein, with historically accurate details.

The narrative begins ca. 1389, when Lazar Hrebeljanović, King of Serbia, was preparing to fend off a formidable invasion by Murad I.

129. His name also appears as Obilić. I have followed the example set by the Count of Sorgo.

130. Bayezid I, second-born son of Murad. He was not yet sultan (emperor), a title proclaimed only after the Battle of Kosovo.

131. Now Montenegro.

But Vukasava, wife of Miloš, laughed at them and cried, "Enough of your boasting, poor little sisters of mine! Speak not to me of Vuk Branković, no renowned knight he. Speak not to me of Đurađ Stracimirović, neither a hero nor a hero's son. Speak instead of Miloš Kobilić, the noble from Novi Pazar. A hero's son is he, birthed by a mother from Herzegovina!"[132]

This irked Branković's wife, and she struck Vukasava across the face. It was a gentle slap, yet blood gushed from her nose.[133]

Young Vukasava sprang to her feet and returned, in tears, to her white palace. Still crying, she called for Miloš and calmly told him this: "Do you know, my lord, my beloved, what Branković's wife said? That you are neither a noble nor a noble's son, but a scoundrel and a scoundrel's son. Branković's wife is boasting still, saying that you would not dare face her lord Branković on the field of honor, for your right hand is lacking in courage."

Miloš, embittered by these words, sprang to his courageous feet, mounted his warhorse, and called for Vuk Branković.

"Vuk Branković, my friend," he said, "if you are born of woman, come with me to the field of honor and let us see which of us is more valiant."

Vuk had no choice but to comply. He mounted his warhorse and rode out over the even plain to the jousting field.[134]

There the two men took up their lances and galloped toward each other, but the lances shattered into pieces. They drew the sabers that hung at their sides, but the sabers, too, broke apart. And so they struck one another with their heavy maces, and the quills were blown away.[135] Fortune favored Miloš, and he disarmed Vuk Branković.

Miloš Kobilić said, "Boast now, Vuk Branković! Go and boast to your loyal wife. Tell her I dare not joust with you. I could kill

---

132. In reality, Miloš was of unknown extraction and rose to prominence as a result of his exploits.

133. According to some accounts, it was Vukasava who struck Mara.

134. The duel was authorized by Lazar.

135. Here, *quills* are understood to mean the iron spikes at the ends of maces.

you now, Vuk, and dress your beloved wife in black! But I will not kill you, for we are friends. Go with God and cease your boasting."

A short time passed, and Lazar was beset by the Turks, led by Sultan Murad. They pillaged; they burned towns and villages. Lazar, unable to endure the devastation they wrought, gathered his army. He called upon Vuk Branković, and he called upon the hero Miloš Kobilić.

He prepared a feast fit for princes, for princes they were. When all had drunk their fill of wine, he addressed the assembled lords and said, "Hear me, warriors; hear me, dukes and princes, my proven heroes. Tomorrow we shall attack the Turks. We shall follow the orders of Miloš Kobilić. For Miloš is a valiant knight, feared by Turks and Christians alike. He shall lead the army as its voivode,[136] and second to him shall be Vuk Branković."

Vuk, embittered by these words, could no longer stand the sight of Miloš. He called to Lazar and spoke to him in secret.

"My good and gentle lord," Vuk said, "you do not realize it, but you have gathered your soldiers in vain! Miloš Kobilić has betrayed you and betrayed his faith; he serves the Turk."

Lazar made no reply; but at the end of the supper, Lazar drank from the golden bowl. His tears flowed in an urgent stream, and he spoke softly. "Neither to the tsar nor to the kaiser,[137] but to my son-in-law Kobilić, who seeks to betray me as Judas betrayed his creator!"

Miloš Kobilić swore by the Almighty that there was no room in his heart for treason or bad faith. He sprang to his courageous feet and returned to his white tents. Until midnight he wept; after midnight he prayed to God.

At the first light of dawn, when the morning star showed its face, he mounted his finest horse and galloped to the sultan's camp. Miloš begged the guards to let him enter the sultan's tent, saying, "I will deliver Lazar's army to him; I will place Lazar, alive, in his hands."

---

136. Commanding general.

137. Presumably, toasts began with the king, followed by the emperor of Germany.

The Turks believed Kobilić and led him to the sultan's feet. Miloš knelt on the black earth and kissed the hem of the sultan's gown. He kissed, too, the sultan's knees. Suddenly he took hold of his khanjar and thrust it into Murad's heart. Then he drew the saber that hung at his side and slashed the pashas and the viziers.[138]

But he, too, suffered a cruel fate, for the Turks cut him into pieces with their sabers. For Vuk Branković's actions, for what he did, may he answer before God!

---

138. Murad survived long enough to learn of his victory in the Battle of Kosovo.

Accounts of his death differ from author to author. Some say that, following the Serbs' defeat, the sultan was walking on the battlefield and was surprised to note the extraordinary youth of the Christians whose bodies were strewn across the Kosovo field. "Only youthful fools," said one of his viziers, "would dare face your weapons." One injured Serb recognized the sultan. He managed, through desperate effort, to stand up and give the sultan a fatal wound with his dagger. He was summarily slaughtered by the Janissaries.

It is said, based on the version in which Murad dies by Miloš's hand, that the tradition of ambassadors appearing unarmed in the presence of Ottoman emperors dates to that event. General Sébastiani was, I believe, the first to refuse to remove his sword, when he was presented to Sultan Selim III.

Vuk Branković delivered the corps he commanded to the Turks. Lazar fought bravely, but his dapple-gray horse ran off and was taken by the enemy, who paraded him triumphantly through their ranks. Seeing this, the Serbs believed their king to be dead or captured, upon which they lost their courage and disbanded. With no possibility of victory, Lazar was captured alive. Shortly thereafter, Bayezid ordered his throat slit, offering him as a sacrifice to the ancestors in his father's honor.

It is claimed that Miloš Kobilić's right hand, set in silver, was fixed to Murad's tomb.

Foreword

[To the 1840 Edition][1]

Around the year of our Lord 1827, I was a romanticist. To the classicists we said, "There is nothing Greek about your Greeks, nothing Roman about your Romans. You fail to imbue your compositions with local color. No glory without local color!" By *local color*, we merely meant what was known, in the seventeenth century, as *social customs*; even so, we took great pride in our term and believed ourselves to have invented both the term and the thing itself. With respect to poetry, we reserved our admiration for foreign poems, the older the better. The Scottish border ballads and the romances of El Cid struck us as masterpieces beyond compare—again, due to their local color.

I longed to go and observe local color where it still existed, as it is not to be found everywhere. Alas, I lacked but one travel necessity: money. As it costs nothing to come up with plans, though, my friends and I devised many.

Those lands most frequented by tourists were not the ones we longed to see. Jean-Jacques Ampère and I sought to avoid the itineraries frequented by the English; thus, after brief stops in Florence, Rome, and Naples, we were to embark at Venice for Trieste and, from there, take a leisurely course along the Adriatic Sea to the city of Ragusa. Indeed, it was the most ingenious, most brilliant, and most novel of plans—save for the matter of money! Seeking to remedy that issue, we had the idea to write our travel tale in advance, sell it at a lucrative price, and use the proceeds to

---

1. Publisher's Note: This Foreword was originally included in the 1840 edition of *La Guzla, ou Choix de poésies illyriques recueillies dans la Dalmatie, la Bosnie, la Croatie et l'Herzégowine*. It is reproduced here at the end of the work, along with the following Translator's Note, so as not to "spoil the fun" of those encountering this text for the first time.

find out whether or not our descriptions were accurate. It was an innovative gambit, but sadly, we gave it up.

In the course of this project, which provided us with amusement for a time, Ampère, who speaks all the languages of Europe, gave me the task—I could not say why, ignorant as I am—of gathering the original poetry of the Illyrians. In preparation, I read Abbe Alberto Fortis' *Travels into Dalmatia*, as well as a rather good statistical analysis of the former Illyrian Provinces, written, if I am not mistaken, by a head clerk at the Foreign Ministry. I learned five or six Slavic words and, in the space of a fortnight, wrote the collection of ballads you hold in your hands.

It was printed in Strasbourg, shrouded in mystery, accompanied by footnotes and a portrait of the "author." My secret was well kept, and the success was tremendous.

True, barely a dozen copies were sold, and to this day, my heart bleeds at the thought of the unfortunate publisher who paid the price for this hoax.[2] However, while the French did not bother to read my work at all, foreigners and qualified experts did me justice.

Two months after the publication of *La Guzla*, Mr. Bowring, who had published an anthology of Slavic verse, wrote to ask me for the original poems that I had translated so well.

Then, Mr. Gerhard, a businessman and scholar from somewhere in Germany, sent me two thick volumes of Slavic poetry translated into German, and *La Guzla* translated in verse—a simple task, he wrote in his preface, as he had uncovered the original meter of the Illyrian poetry beneath my prose. The Germans do have a well-known knack for uncovering things! This particular German asked me for more ballads from which to craft a third volume.

Finally, Mr. Pushkin translated a few of my little stories into Russian, which is akin to seeing *Gil Blas* translated into Spanish or the *Letters of a Portuguese Nun* translated into Portuguese.

Brilliant though this success may have been, it did not go to my head. Gratified by the corroboration of Messrs. Bowring, Gerhard,

---

2. Publisher's Note: The present publisher of this work commiserates across time and space with the original publisher of this work.

and Pushkin, I could pride myself on having created local color; but doing so had been so simple, so easy, that I came to doubt its very merit, and I pardoned Racine for having tamed the rugged heroes of Sophocles and Euripides.

1840.

Translator's Note

Laura Nagle

It isn't often that a translator's note begins with the wildly redundant assertion that the literary work presented as a translation has been translated by a translator. In the case of this book, however, it seems wise to put any lingering doubts to rest. Just so it's clear: I, Laura Nagle, translated *La Guzla* from French into English. By putting my name on *Songs for the Gusle*, I am acknowledging that I have, to the best of my ability and through the inevitable prism of my interpretations, conveyed in English the tone and content of the French-language source text, whose author's name appears above mine on the cover of this book because he is the one who wrote it in the first place.

I promise the above is true. One hundred percent factual. Really.

If you still have your doubts, though, that's only natural. In 1827, when *La Guzla, ou Choix de poésies illyriques recueillies dans la Dalmatie, la Bosnie, la Croatie et l'Herzégowine* was first published, its "translator" made similar claims. He identified himself, though not by name, with copious autobiographical details and assertions of his suitability to translate the ballads presented in the book, which were (he asserted) authentic cultural artifacts he had accumulated in the course of his travels. Some of those songs, he claimed, were the work of one "Hyacinthe Maglanovich," a man whom he had met and interviewed at length; others were of unknown authorship, perhaps handed down through the generations. The remainder of the collected texts were essays he had written in the course of his travels through the Balkans, based on his personal experiences and encounters with speakers of the South Slavic languages he refers to as "Illyrian."

The "translator's" life story, the travel narratives, and the bard Maglanović himself were the fictional creations of Prosper Mérimée, as he acknowledged in his foreword to the 1840 edition of *La Guzla*. In the intervening years, Mérimée had established himself as a master of the novella form: *Mateo Falcone, Tamango*, and *La Vénus d'Ille* were all published during this period. He was soon to follow up those successes with his two best-known novellas, *Colomba* and *Carmen* (made even more famous, a generation later, by Bizet's opera). It might seem at first glance like an odd choice for Mérimée, at that point in his career, to revisit this anonymous early work. It is worth noting that Mérimée's first biographer cast doubt on the veracity of the author's self-deprecating rationalizations, calling the 1840 foreword an additional hoax tacked onto the original one ("une seconde mystification greffée sur celle de 1827").[1]

As it happens, though, *La Guzla* wasn't the only hoax that Mérimée perpetrated when he was a young, unknown civil servant. His first book, published in 1825, was a series of short plays supposedly written by a Spanish actress and presented under her name, Clara Gazul (note that her surname is an anagram of Guzla). His authorship of those texts was an open secret in Parisian literary circles, and the book attracted praise from the likes of Balzac and Goethe. Perhaps, then, it should come as little surprise that Mérimée chose to pursue another "mystification," this time kept under wraps. But how did he settle on folk ballads of the Balkans as the subject matter for his next hoax, and what made him think there was an audience for this type of literature?

Perhaps the biggest clue lies in his use of the term "Illyrian," which Mérimée's contemporaries would recognize without difficulty. Most of the tales in this collection are set in territories—parts of modern-day Croatia, Slovenia, and Italy—that were collectively known as the Illyrian Provinces while under Napoleonic rule (1809–14). In the original 1827 preface, Mérimée's fictional translator declines to describe the region's history or geographic features, as he expects French readers to have ample familiarity

---

1. Augustin Filon, *Mérimée et ses amis* (Paris: Hachette, 1894), pp. 37–38.

with the former Illyrian Provinces. That argument is, of course, disingenuous; the region had been under French control within living memory, but only for a brief period. As Christopher L. Miller notes, "Mérimée's Illyria must have been almost completely unfamiliar to French readers, leaving him free to make up whatever he liked. It was a blank slate, the very opposite of what is stated in the preface."[2]

In other words, Mérimée was undoubtedly aware that his own familiarity with the cultures and history of the Balkans was limited, and he was counting on his readers not to be any better informed. Indeed, the success of his hoax would depend on French readers finding a link between his "authentic ballads" and the equally fictional representations of "Dalmatian improvisers" in the early works of Charles Nodier and in Madame de Staël's novel *Corinne*. Incidentally, Nodier, who spent several months as a librarian and newspaper editor in Ljubljana in 1812–13, appears not even to have realized that Serbo-Croatian and Slovene were different languages; he referred to all the languages spoken in the Illyrian Provinces as one and the same "illyrien."[3]

To Mérimée's apparent surprise, however, *La Guzla* found its most receptive audience outside of France. In addition to Pushkin's partial translation and the efforts of John Bowring and Wilhelm Gerhard mentioned in Mérimée's 1840 foreword, notable early reviewers of *La Guzla* include Goethe and Mary Shelley. While Goethe drew a connection between *La Guzla* and *Théâtre de Clara Gazul* as early as 1828 and Shelley followed suit a year later, many of Mérimée's contemporaries initially took the story of "Hyacinthe Maglanovich" and his anonymous translator at face value.[4]

Even by the standards of nineteenth-century French literature, which was rife with intercultural hoaxes, *La Guzla* was unusually

---

2. Christopher L. Miller, *Impostors: Literary Hoaxes and Cultural Authenticity* (Chicago: The University of Chicago Press, 2018), p. 66.

3. Voyslav M. Yovanovitch [Vojislav M. Jovanović], *"La Guzla" de Prosper Mérimée* (Paris: Hachette, 1911), p. 75.

4. Yovanovitch, pp. 464–65.

successful in convincing readers of its authenticity.[5] No doubt the presence of supposed fragments, paired with anecdotes about the circumstances under which they had been "discovered," served to fool some readers. For others, the plausibility of Mérimée's hoax may have turned on the one genuine South Slavic folk ballad in the collection: *Hasanaginica*, or "The Mourning Song of the Noble Wife of Hasan-Aga." This poem had been published in Italian, German, and English (the best-known versions being translations by Alberto Fortis, Goethe, and Walter Scott, respectively) in the latter decades of the eighteenth century, and its inclusion lent credence to the collection's claims of authenticity.

Indeed, even the knowledge that it was a hoax did not dissuade Mary Shelley from recommending the book on the basis of its consonance with Western Europeans' perceptions of the region: "By a strong effort of the imagination, the young Parisian writes as if the mountains of Illyria had been the home of his childhood; the rustic and barbarous manners are not softened, nor the wild energy of the people tamed; and, if we trace any vestige of civilization, it merely arises from the absence of all that would shock our tastes or prejudices."[6] Even for Mérimée's most discerning peers, "authenticity" seems to have been a matter more of feeling—of conformity with preconceived notions—than of factual accuracy.

Readers today are likely to make different judgments of these stories' plausibility, not only because of our heightened sensitivity to cultural stereotypes but also because we have easy access to a wealth of information. For example, a nineteenth-century reader in France might have had no reason to doubt that a traveler leaving Vrgorac on foot would casually happen upon the town of Vrboska, but a quick online search easily proves otherwise. While I've chosen to employ some archaic language and changed Mérimée's French- and Italian-inflected spellings of names and places so that

---

5. Miller, pp. 51–54 and 59–64.

6. Mary Shelley, "Illyrian Poems – Feudal Scenes," *Westminster Review* 10 (January 1829), pp. 72–73.

they are more congruent with the stories' settings, I cannot expect twenty-first century readers to be fooled by this fakelore for long.

To my mind, the best argument for introducing *La Guzla* to a new audience nearly two centuries after its first publication is not the fakelore but the character of the "translator," whose suspiciously detailed biographies of himself and the gusle player Maglanović ought to have been the first clue to Mérimée's early readers that something was amiss. In the abundant footnotes to his supposed translations, he purports to contextualize the tales with unnecessary, unhelpful, and often misleading "facts" for the benefit of French-speaking readers. It is possible to enjoy reading the ballads on their own, but it is in the interruptions—the basic terms defined for the umpteenth time, or the authoritative-sounding but error-riddled summaries of historical events—that the "translator" emerges as a recognizable character. Convinced of his cultural and intellectual superiority, he does not hesitate to portray himself as an expert. He compulsively inserts his dubious insights into stories whose integrity he claims to value. In lieu of a knowledgeable tour guide, Mérimée has given us an archetypal blowhard.

The circumstances under which *La Guzla* was published and received by its early readers are so extraordinary that they have tended to dominate any mention of the book. Prior English translations of excerpts have generally focused on the fakelore, leaving out the footnotes and thus depriving readers of Mérimée's remarkable portrait of the faux translator. In providing an English translation of the full text for the first time, I hope to offer a new audience the opportunity to untangle *La Guzla*'s threads of fact, fiction, and satire.

ABOUT THE AUTHOR

Prosper Mérimée (1803–1870), a French writer and translator from Russian, was a major figure in the Romantic movement. He is remembered as a pioneer of the novella, with *Carmen* (1845) and *Colomba* (1840) figuring among his best-known works. A noted archaeologist and advocate for historic preservation, Mérimée served for two decades as France's inspector-general of historic monuments.

ABOUT THE TRANSLATOR

Laura Nagle is a translator and writer based in Indianapolis. Her translations of prose and poetry from French and Spanish have appeared in journals including *AGNI*, *The Southern Review*, ANMLY, and *The Los Angeles Review*. She received a Travel Fellowship from the American Literary Translators Association in 2020.

ABOUT THE [illegible]

Prosper Mérimée (18[illegible]) [illegible] of Russian [illegible] is remembered as [illegible] (1840) [illegible]

[illegible]

[illegible] THE [illegible]

[illegible]

CPSIA information can be obtained
at www.ICGtesting.com
Printed in the USA
BVHW030234221122
652488BV00007B/181